FRAME UP

FRAME UP

A NOVEL

JAMES PHOENIX

GREY SWAN PRESS

Publisher of Fine Books   Marblehead, Massachusetts

First Edition: September 2012
Published by Grey Swan Press
Marblehead, MA 01945
www.greyswanpress.com

100% acid-free paper
Printed in the United States

First Edition

Library of Congress Control Number: 2012939396

ISBN: 978-0-9834900-3-6

0 9 8 7 6 5 4 3 2 1

For Susan,
bright, beautiful, warm, loving,
thrifty, kind and reverent ... my
true inspiration and the great love
of my life.

"Sure, I have advice for people starting to write. Don't. I don't need the competition."

Robert B. Parker

"Parker had no competition. My writing may resemble but will never match his genius. Still, I try."

James Phoenix

CHAPTER 1

I was pouring myself a beer and plugging *Casablanca* into the DVD player when Tiny Dan Murphy pounded on the steel hull of my floating home. The *Queen Anne's Revenge* is a fifty-eight foot sloop in need of a good coat of paint. She is berthed in Marblehead Harbor, right in the middle of a dozen other first-class craft in much better shape. Dan's heavy hand made it sound like I was inside a bell tower, with the ringer working overtime.

The dogs went nuts. I've got two of them, English mastiffs. Delicate little flowers: Rowlf weighs in at two hundred thirty-eight pounds with a thirty-two inch neck; his girlfriend Blanche, a real lady, comes in at two-twelve. Her water bowl is half the size of a standard bathtub. Letters on the side read: "I have always relied on the kindness of strangers, but even when they aren't kind, it still works out well." Below that, in bold italics: ***"Cause then I get to eat them."***

"Easy, big man," I shouted. I didn't have to ask who it was.

"Permission to come aboard, sir!" Dan shouted. He jumped up on deck and offered the dogs the customary treats. Their tails wagged like bullwhips. I was careful to step out of the way. I'm six-foot-three, but Tiny—as just about everyone called Dan—stands a head taller and is twice as wide. He has a full beard and a thick head of blazing red hair. Overall, he's a hard guy to miss. Among his other interests, Tiny runs the largest bookie operation in New England. Whitey Bulger and his heirs run Boston's organized crime, but they give Tiny a wide berth and he's kind of a prince in his own right.

"Morning, Fenway," he said. "Halfway expected to find you sleeping in."

I looked at my watch; just after eleven. "Nah, been up close to an hour. Don't have any popcorn, but I got an old movie in the DVD. Care to join me, have a couple of beers?"

"Little early in the day, isn't it? Even for you," Tiny said.

"Not a whole lot going on at the moment."

Tiny nodded. "*Casablanca*?"

"Must be psychic."

"How many times you seen it, anyway?"

I shrugged. "Got no idea. Great flick though. You've seen it."

"Parts of it, but I didn't come down here to watch a black-and-white. Shut the damn thing off and I'll buy ya lunch. Little business we need to talk about. "

"You're buying?"

"Invited you, didn't I?"

"You're on."

I threw back my beer and we headed for *Maddie's* up on

State Street, right around the corner from my berth on the dock. It's a regular Marblehead institution with pressed tin ceilings and a battered wooden bar that has been there since before the Flood. The place has more characters than *War & Peace*. Whiff Abbott is among the most colorful of these. He sat at the bar. A bit early for lunch, the old lobsterman had the place to himself. He's just over five-foot-six, with an unkempt white beard halfway down to his belt buckle. Whiff practically raised me since I lost my dad at twelve.

He waved and smiled as we came in, exposing ragged, yellow choppers. Whiff had more than twenty boats in the water, but ran his finances old school: no sense giving some dentist money while he could still chew.

"Well, as I live and breathe, the Gold Dust twins!" He rose on unsteady legs.

I looked to the bartender. "How long's he been in here, Doug?"

"Don't know. Didn't get in 'til nine myself."

"I see."

Whiff pointed to a booth. "You boys up for lunch? I'm buying."

"You're on," Tiny said. "Figured I'd be stuck with the tab."

"What? You mean the big-shot private eye here? He ain't tight, just got to catch him when he's got money in his pocket."

I turned to Tiny. "You had some business you wanted to talk about, didn't you?"

Whiff held up his hands. "Didn't mean to stick my nose in." He turned back to the bar.

"That's OK, Whiff," Tiny said. "Nothing I'm afraid to say in front of you. Especially if you're buying."

Whiff came to the booth. "You sure?"

Tiny nodded. "Have a seat. Little favor is all, it's my Ma."

"Your Ma's in trouble with the law? You got to be—"

Tiny cut him off. "It's her friend's son. Punk kid two years at Walpole."

"What's the rap?" I said.

"Murder. Doing life; says he had nothing to do with it."

"There's a surprise," I said. "And you want him out?"

"Just like you to nose around is all. That is, if you're ready to finally get off your ass."

"Was taking a little time off. Couple bucks in my back pocket with my half of the divorce settlement."

"So you'll take a look?"

"I'll take a look."

"I'll have the transcripts from the trial in your hands by tonight. That'll do for a start. Give you a little reading material to keep you out of trouble."

"Delightful."

"Oh, and I might as well tell you right now, they got three eyewitnesses saying they saw him pull the trigger, then drive off in a Lincoln."

"Anything else?"

"Been arrested something like forty-five times. Quite an accomplishment; he just turned twenty-one last week."

"Uh huh. And my fee?"

"Yeah. Might have to wait a while on that. His mother rents a third floor apartment over in Dorchester."

"Well, there's something, at least. Money's no object."

"No object at all."

Whiff waved to the bartender. "Lobsters all around, and three pitchers of your finest!" Things were looking up.

CHAPTER 2

I have an old Boston cop contact working out of Corbett's district. That'd be as good a place to start as any. I'd never worked Dorchester when I was on the force. But I knew Dolan was the man I had to see. He was a Boston detective working vice before he got promoted. Dolan is a captain now, with a beet-red face and the start of a gut. We caught up on old times, and then I asked him about Tiny's little pal, a Mr. Shawn Corbett.

"Corbett, yeah, I know him all right, pinched him myself a dozen times. What about him?" Dolan spoke with the raspy voice of a heavy smoker.

"Taking another look at his case."

"Some new evidence come to light or something?"

"Nope."

Dolan gave me a look.

"Checking around. The family thinks it was a setup," I added.

"There were three witnesses, weren't there?"

"So they tell me," I said.

"Best of luck to you."

Can you tell me anything about him?"

Dolan sighed. "Little twist, but the same old story: dropped out of school early, break-ins, peddling dope, worked with one of Whitey Bulger's boys. Did some collecting for a shark, in and out of juvie."

"What's the twist?"

"Kid actually had some family who cared about him. Didn't do him any good, though. He's a punk, period."

"You think he killed that student in Lynn."

"Convicted, isn't he? I'm not shedding any tears he's locked up."

"Claims he had nothing to do with it," I said.

"Yeah, yeah, happens all the time." He stood up and went to the window. "Come 'ere." The street was lined on both sides with battered cars, eight to ten years old, some with wheels missing. There were three-decker wooden tenements, half of them looking like they hadn't been painted since the early fifties. Kids on the sidewalk. All white boys here—not a great plan for any black kid to put in an appearance in this neighborhood. But hip-hop was alive and well in working-class Irish Dorchester, and the kids all wore the same uniform: oversized jeans, and tops, Boston Red Sox hats at off angles, even a do-rag here and there.

"All those kids, they'll get set up too, one way or another. Every one of 'em innocent. It's a conspiracy's, what it is."

What could I say? I just kept my mouth shut.

"He belongs on the inside," Dolan said.

"Maybe."

"'Maybe' my ass, kid's no fucking good. You know that as well as I do. You met this Corbett kid yet?"

"He's next on my list."

"Then you'll see exactly what I mean. You're in for a real experience, you are."

CHAPTER 3

It was drizzling. Tiny and I took a road trip out to the Cedar Junction Correctional Institution in Walpole. It was impossible for him to get comfortable in my little antique Porsche, and we were more than a bit cramped. "Jesus, you ever think of getting a real car?" Tiny asked.

"What can I tell ya, it runs and it's got a lot of character. The chicks go wild."

"What year is this thing anyway?"

"Older than both of us: 1956 Porsche Speedster."

"Might want to consider a new top; getting wet in here."

"On the list."

We stopped for coffee at the Starbucks in Reading, just off Route 128. Tiny picked up a half-dozen maple frosted scones and managed to make a royal mess of himself in the car. He offered me one, but didn't repeat the offer and went to work on the rest as I sipped my black *venti* French roast.

"Anything special jump out at you in the transcripts?" he asked between bites. There were crumbs all over his windbreaker.

"You mean besides the murder weapon and the vic's wallet being found in my guy's apartment? You didn't tell me about those."

"Kid said it wasn't his."

"Right."

Neither one of us said anything for a while. I was having a hard time seeing the road, and made a mental note to get some new windshield wipers.

"His previous record came out. Never should have," I said.

"Public defender."

"Prejudicial," I said.

"You think? Just wait till you get a load of this guy. I'll show you prejudicial."

By the time we got to Cedar Junction the rain was coming down in buckets. The sky was gunmetal gray, and the prison's stonewalls looked medieval.

We went though five checkpoints on the way to the visiting room. At each stop, we had to present our visitor IDs while the guards gave us the once-over. Eventually, we reached the last stop.

"Daniel Murphy and Fenway Burke," the guard said, handing us back our IDs. He was an older guy, a little taller than me, with his gut hanging over his buckle. "Follow me." He unlocked the heavy metal door to a small windowless room. A bull-necked man with a shaved head sat inside. The table he was chained to was bolted to the floor. Every inch of exposed skin was covered with tattoos.

"Gentlemen, meet Shawn Corbett. He's all yours."

Corbett gave us a poisonous look. I turned to Tiny. "He's got a spider web tattooed on his face."

"No foolin'," Tiny said.

We sat across from him. "I'm Fenway Burke," I said. "This is—"

"I know who he is," Corbett said, then nodded to Tiny. "What's this all about?"

"About getting you out." Tiny said. "Fenway's a private investigator."

Corbett snorted.

I stood up. "You don't want to cooperate?" I said.

Corbett shook his head. "Nah, nah." He tried to motion for me to sit back down but his chains wouldn't let him. "I didn't do it," he said. "But I ain't going nowhere."

I sat back down. "Tell me what happened," I said.

"Not much to tell. I'm having a beer in my apartment, cops come busting in and drag me out to Lynn, put me in solitary."

"You had no idea what it was all about?" I said.

"Thought it was a drug bust. Used to deal a little."

"But then they took you out of Boston," I said.

"Yeah, I knew something was up."

"You ever been to Lynn?" I said.

"Nope," Corbett said.

"It's only fifteen miles away," Tiny said.

Corbett just shrugged.

"They found a nine millimeter Glock. You know anything about that?" I asked.

"Not mine. Had a thirty-eight under a floorboard. They

never found it."

I nodded. "You got a friend with a gray Lincoln?"

Corbett frowned and shook his head.

"Credit cards, did you have any?" I said.

"Never had no bank account," Corbett said.

"They had three witnesses pick you out of a lineup. How do you explain that?" I asked.

"Frame up, like I told you. I was never there."

"You figure there's dark forces at work trying to put Shawn Corbett away for life?"

Corbett's eyes narrowed. "This ain't no joke," he said.

I grilled him for almost an hour, but got nothing. I leaned back in my chair.

"You got anything else you want to tell me?" I said.

Corbett shook his head. "You ain't listening. I'm telling ya ... I had nothing to do with it. Get it? It's a frame up."

🔫 🔫 🔫

THE PORSCHE STARTED HARD, but she always did in the rain.

"So, what'd you think?" Tiny asked.

"Lot of damn work that'll more than likely lead nowhere."

"More 'n likely, but I need you to check it out. Really check it out."

"Haven't done much of anything since the divorce," I said.

"I noticed," Tiny said. "You 'bout ready to rejoin the human race?"

I put her in gear and pulled out of the parking lot. "Good a time as any," I said.

Tiny reached into his jacket and then handed me a check. "Don't expect you to work for free."

I looked it over, nodded, and put it in my pocket.

"Thought I'd have to chase the kid's family for my fee."

Tiny shook his head. "Nah, I got you covered."

"What the hell do you care about this guy?"

Tiny didn't say anything for a moment. "Long story. Don't really want to talk about it right now. You in, or do I have to get someone else?"

"I'm in," I said.

Tiny grunted a response.

"No guarantees, you know that. I go wherever the facts lead me."

"Just so you work it hard."

"I will," I said.

Tiny nodded, leaned back and closed his eyes as I accelerated down the street.

"I do have a couple of questions," I said.

"Yeah?"

"The murder weapon for one thing: 9 millimeter Glock G-17, seventeen shots in the magazine. Got to be at least twenty-five hundred on the street. High-end for that guy."

"True."

"He got busted in Lynn."

"So?"

"He's got no car. How'd he get there? The last MBTA's stop is 'Wonderland.'"

"They'll just say he stole it," Tiny said.

"No gray Lincoln reported stolen."

"A friend's, maybe."

"He's got a friend with a late model Lincoln?" I said. "I'm checking it out, but that sound likely?"

Tiny skipped a beat. "Might have rented it."

"You need a credit card to rent a car. You figure he used his American Express Platinum? Didn't take a cab, already checked the logs, nothing to Oxford Street in Lynn all night."

"Right, so now what?"

"Check it out, what else?" I said.

Tiny nodded. "Good man."

"It's what I do. Anyway, nice day for a drive.

It started to rain again, and the windshield began to fog. I reached over and cleared it as well as I could. The fan on the defroster needed a new fuse.

Tiny hiked up his collar as the rain started to leak in just over his head.

CHAPTER 4

I'd paid rent on my little office for six months but had never actually been there since moving the furniture in. It wasn't much, just a single room with a couple of chairs facing an old metal desk. But it did have my name on the door: Fenway Burke, Private Investigator. I booted up the computer but was unable to log on. The phone line was dead. I made a note to call Verizon and headed out the door. I had people to see.

Detective Charlie Quinn didn't bother to get up from his desk as I came in. Mid-thirties, he was short and built like a fire hydrant. It was just after nine in the morning, but he already had a five o'clock shadow. In fact, the black stubble on his checks was about the same as his head. I started to speak but he cut me off.

"You got to be Burke. Somebody said you wanted to talk to me."

"He tell you why?"

"Old case of mine. I collar a lot of scum balls, but that guy I remember. God damn animal: rolls a music student, then blows his brains out, open and shut. I hear you're trying to get him off."

"Mind if I ask a few questions?"

"No problem. I love it when some asshole rattles my cage. Three eyewitnesses saw him pull the trigger. We got the murder weapon, found the victim's wallet in his apartment, half the loot gone. What else you want?"

"What pointed you to Corbett?"

"Anonymous letter. It's all in the transcripts."

"Read about it. Public-spirited citizen?"

"Undoubtedly."

"Got any idea who sent it?"

"What the fuck difference does that make?"

"Right, you must get a lot of hot tips like that, makes your job a regular breeze."

"I get shit, but things got a way of coming out. Look it, I ain't got all day, okay. You got anything else?" He started leafing through a pile of papers on his desk.

"So you had his name and address. You just breezed in and busted him?"

"Shoulda seen that rathole he was living in, just off Columbus Avenue. Stank like hell of cat piss. Only he didn't have no cat."

"Nice. The witnesses, they came forward after his arrest?"

"Not so unusual."

"You think?"

Quinn stood up. "You seen that guy?"

"I admit he's not refined."

"He's a fucking cannibal, for Christ's sake. All he needs is a bone through his nose."

"Just want to make sure the guy's getting a fair shake. Kind of a family thing, pal of mine's halfway related to the mother."

"He's got a mother?"

"He's got a mother."

Quinn got red in the face. "Listen: do yourself a favor. Keep your nose out of my cases. Leave it alone. Got it?"

I stood. "Thanks so much for your time, Detective."

Quinn looked like he wanted to make a move on me but didn't. His phone rang. He picked it up before it could ring again.

"Yeah? Yeah, yeah, on my way." He fumbled through the papers on his desk. "Got the deposition right here." He hung up and scanned the paperwork. I could see his lips moving. I showed myself out.

CHAPTER 5

I was sound asleep when I heard someone clambering around on deck. The dogs started barking. I cursed and looked at the blue light of my digital clock: 4:38.

"Who the hell's up there?" I yelled, still half asleep.

"Who the hell ya think?" my guest shouted back.

The dogs instantly stopped barking and wagged their tails at Whiff's familiar voice. I shook my head and rubbed my eyes. "You drunk?" I shouted.

The hatch opened and he stuck his head down.

"Nah, not yet anyway," he said. "Working day for me and we got ta talk."

I looked at him from the bed.

"Well," Whiff said.

"It's not even five."

"Yeah, well ... life starts early in my business. Get some clothes on and I'll buy ya a cup of coffee."

"What's this all about?" I said.

"Nothing much, just your life is all."

"I—"

"Never mind all the bullshit. We'll talk on board. Got the *Lovely Edna* warming up right now."

"We pulling traps?" I asked.

"Among other things, yeah. Come on. I ain't got all day."

"Got some work to do," I said.

"So get to it later. I need you *now*."

He left me there, still in bed. I heard him jump off the deck like a much younger man and head down the pier to the *Lovely Edna*. I gave myself a minute and then climbed out of bed and put some clothes on. What the hell. Whatever he wanted, it wasn't likely to take all day.

He was casting off the lines as I jumped on board. The boat started to move under my feet as I hit the deck. I lost my balance for a second and grabbed the rail for support. Whiff was at the wheel.

"Coffee's on below, grab us both a cup," he said with his eyes straight ahead. He threaded her out of the crowded harbor to the open ocean. I joined him on deck. We both sipped our coffee, neither one of us saying anything. That seemed okay somehow.

About a mile offshore and we were in the middle of Whiff's lobster buoys. With his distinctive red and bright yellow stripes, they were easy to spot. Whiff turned the wheel hard and came up right beside one. I knew what to do; as a kid, I'd worked summers on his boats. I grabbed the pole with the hook on the end and snagged the trap line, then slipped it into the electric hoist and flipped the switch ... nothing. I flipped it again, still nothing.

Whiff laughed. "Been meaning ta get that fixed," he said.

"So I've got to pull these traps by hand? You got to be kidding me!"

"'Bout time ya made an honest dollar. Haul away."

"Right." I started in on the rope hand-over-hand. Felt like I was raising the Titanic.

We spent the morning going from one buoy to the next. I tried to draw him out but all Whiff talked about was how the catch had dropped off over the years and how nobody wanted to work anymore. By ten-thirty, my arms were trembling and the muscles in my upper back were starting to rebel. I'd had it.

"You going to tell me what the hell I'm doing out here or what?" I said.

Whiff opened the hopper and looked in at our catch.

"Good a time as any," he said, then turned off the engine and pointed the boat to a trap opposite his stool at the wheel. There was no sound but the water lapping on the old wooden hull. The *Lovely Edna* rocked gently.

"Have a seat," he said. He didn't say anything at first but just looked down at his hands.

"Well." I said.

He looked up and gave me a tired smile.

"Went to the doc," he said.

"Whiff—"

"I ain't dead yet."

"What's the—"

"Prostate cancer's done a little spreading. They got it under control, but it got me thinking. Hell, I'm eighty-two years old. No one lives forever."

"Guess not," I said. "So you figured you'd take it out on me by breaking my back, is that it?"

Whiff chuckled. "You're on to me," he said. "But while I got ya out here anyway, I figured I'd offer you a chance to take over my business. Regular going concern, twenty boats and all of 'em turning a buck."

"Don't know what to say," I said.

"You're the closest thing to family I got."

"Goes both ways," I said.

He nodded. Neither one of us said anything for a while. The sun came out from behind the clouds. It felt hot on my back, but a pleasant hot.

"To be honest, I'm not entirely sure just what I want to do with the rest of my life."

"Knew you'd say that," Whiff said. He stood up and patted me on the back.

"Like I say, I ain't dead yet. Just think it over. Fair enough?"

"Yeah, Whiff, fair enough."

CHAPTER 6

It turned out that Megan Griffin, the public defender who handled Corbett's case, lived right in Marblehead and was a member of the Marblehead Athletic Club. I gave her a call. She had a full calendar, but agreed to meet me there. She was taking an aerobics class.

I held the heavy bag as Tiny hammered away. He wasn't what you'd call fancy, but every time he hit it, he just about tore the damn thing right off the chain. I filled him in on my meeting with Quinn as he was pounding away, working up a good lather. Then it was my turn on the bag. He held on tight as I started in with my usual routine, a rapid series of chops followed by high roundhouse kicks. You could hear the rhythmic thuds all over the gym.

"Guy sounds like a real hard ass," Tiny said.

"Didn't expect him to give me a kiss; no cop likes opening a closed case."

Tiny took a little break, grabbed a towel and wiped his brow. "You think there's any kind of chance at another trial?" he said.

"Way too early to tell. Might be able to claim ineffective counsel, but it's a long shot."

"Yeah?"

"His record never should have come up, but a new trial would be a waste of time. Only way to get him off would be a confession by someone else. You read the transcript?" I asked.

"Figured that's what I was paying you for," Tiny said.

"Had to gag him through most of the trial, kept screaming obscenities. Finally they take the gag off before the judge is about to sentence him. The kid gets his chance to speak but just glares at her, not a word. He's handcuffed, remember, but somehow he manages to whip his dick out and wave it at her."

"Got to give him points for style," Tiny said.

I was just finishing my kicks when the door opened, and I saw our new arrival out of the corner of my eye. I stood there, out of breath, and just looked at her. She was close to six feet tall and wore shiny pink shorts and a white top. A pink headband held back shoulder-length auburn hair. She had olive skin, bright eyes that were more gold than green, with full lips and a narrow, delicate nose.

"Are you Fenway Burke?" she said with a smile that lit up her whole face and exposed perfect white teeth.

For a moment, I simply couldn't think of anything to say. It was, after all, a complicated question.

"Well?"

I came to. "I'm sorry, yes, I am he." I smiled and offered my hand. "And this is my little pal, Danny Murphy."

"Megan Griffin. I'm running late. Could we talk maybe after my class?"

"Of course," I said.

She pointed to the bag. You're not one of those cage fighters are you, Mr. Burke?"

"Fenway," I said. "Not my thing at all. Got a couple black belts, but I just can't get around the idea of hitting a man when he's down."

"You nuts? That's the best time to hit him," Tiny said

"Well, you certainly look like you know what you're doing," she said.

Absurd, but I turned bright red. She smiled and I felt my ears burning. It was like being in high school all over again. Tiny picked up on it right off, then looked away and tried to fade into the woodwork.

The door opened and a half-dozen women entered, followed by the instructor.

"I've got to hit the showers. Buy you a cup of coffee after your workout, if you like. Starbucks?" I asked.

"Of course; you'll never get me into a Dunkin' Donuts."

"Perish the thought."

r   r   r

MEGAN CAME INTO STARBUCKS a few minutes after I got there, still in her workout gear. Every head in the joint turned, and not to ogle me. I waved and she joined me at my table. She refused even a bite of my maple scone, so I bought her a fat-free vanilla macchiato, whatever the hell that is. I sipped a black French roast.

"I was right out of law school when I took your client's case.

I'm afraid I didn't do much to help him. You read the transcripts, I assume," Megan said.

"I was surprised his record came out."

She lowered her eyes. "My fault. I was brand new and didn't raise an objection until it was too late. The judge told the jury to disregard it, but—"

"It was already out there."

"Exactly."

Neither one of us said anything for a while.

"My boss wanted a plea bargain, but Corbett insisted on a trial."

"You sure you don't want to reconsider," I said, offering her a bit of my scone. She hesitated a minute and then took it. "Did you think he had any kind of a chance?"

"They had some incredibly damning evidence, but I didn't like the way it matched up with his record. There's nothing but petty stuff, the sort of thing you'd expect from a street punk, mostly drug-related, public intoxication, disorderly conduct, possession with intent to sell, and not a single arrest out of the neighborhood."

"Don't forget assault," I said. "Nine arrests."

"I'm not saying he isn't frightening, but he is from Dorchester, not Marblehead. Is there anything else?"

I thought about it for a moment. "Yes, as a matter of fact. I've got the trial transcripts, but I need file photos on all the evidence presented. Can you help me out on that?"

She nodded. "I'm just wrapping up a case. Is tomorrow night all right?"

"Appreciate that," I said. "I'll match the photos up with what I find at the crime scene. Do you have a card?"

She reached inside her oversized purse, rummaged around a bit and finally found one. "I don't have any pockets," she said.

"I noticed." I took the card. "We could do drinks, dinner maybe?"

A smile played on the corners of her lips. "Professionally?"

I laughed. "Well, a girl's got to eat."

She laughed. "This Fenway thing, a nickname?"

"Nope, was born with it."

She gave me a look.

"Blame it on my Gramps, guy was a nut about the Sox. My parents folded."

"Are you a nut too?"

"Can't name more than two players on the team."

"That's a relief."

"You're not a Sox fan?"

"Of course I am, but there are other things in life."

"No argument."

She smiled, reached over and took her card back, and wrote something on the back.

"My cell."

This was turning into a productive day.

CHAPTER 7

Dingy was the word. Downtown Lynn's salad days had long since passed. Market Street was a ghost town, littered with boarded-up store fronts, pawn shops and check-cashing stores. The once-booming shoe factories had closed their doors years ago, first taking the jobs south, then to Asia. The city's biggest employer, General Electric, had cut its work force by close to ninety-eight percent. Still, the old girl was starting to show signs of life. Just twelve miles north of Boston, luxury condos were popping up here and there. The Lynn Mattress Factory was the first and most successful. The lofts featured fifteen-foot beamed ceilings, exposed brick, and great ocean views from the upper floors. Eighty-five percent of the units sold out in the first few weeks. Of course it was right next to a homeless shelter, but that situation was fluid. Just ask any real estate agent.

There was still no real shopping, but there were a half-dozen upscale bars and restaurants catering to the newly gentrified residents. The Other Side was on Oxford Street. There were hanging plants and a lot of glass, bright and airy with a long mahogany bar. Various reduction sauces were on the menu—a far cry from the shot-and-beer joint that had been the previous tenant.

The body of Nicholas Simpson, Corbett's alleged victim, had been found in the alley right next door. I didn't expect any evidence from a two-year-old crime scene, but I nosed around anyway, just to be sure. I moved some trash barrels, then took out my tape measure. Using the crime scene photos as a guide, I drew my own chalk outline and double-checked the distance from the brick wall.

The vic was face-down in the photo; the shots had knocked him into the wall, slamming the back of his head into it. He had bounced back onto his face. I felt the grimy surface of the wall as a rat ran over my feet, startling me. Bingo, three pock marks, unmistakably bullet holes. I brushed them as clean as I could and took some pictures up close, measuring exactly how high up on the wall they were. Then I pulled the file photo and checked the angle at which they'd hit the body. It looked to be straight on and about level with my chest. The shooter had been tall, six feet at least, and from where the bullets entered the body, more than likely left-handed.

I opened Corbett's file and frowned: six-foot-one and, naturally, left-handed. Not exactly what I'd been hoping for.

I measured off the distance from were the witnesses had been standing. I had to admit it made sense: they would have been close enough to finger the triggerman, even in the dark. I decided I'd come back after nightfall and check out the lighting, just to be sure.

It was 5:00 p.m. and still slow at the bar. I looked at the drink menu: a dozen metrosexual martinis, all with vodka, anything from strawberries and some sort of crème liquor to key lime pie and graham cracker dipped on the rim of the glass, to God-knows-what. The bartender was Asian, with spiked black hair and a silk shirt open almost to the navel. Guy couldn't have weighed ninety pounds. He gave me a smile.

"May I help you, sir?"

I put down the drink menu and smiled back. "You're dazzling me here, but why don't I try the strawberry one."

"The mojito or the martini?"

"Surprise me."

"I'll make you a martini. It's a favorite of mine," he said.

He made quite a show of it, first shaking it over his left shoulder, then his right before pouring it into an oversized, long-stemmed, martini glass with a green swirl just under the base. He placed it in front of me and waited for me to take my first sip.

"Satisfactory?"

It tasted like a lollypop. "Yes, fine, just fine," I said.

He smiled and leaned over the bar. "Haven't seen you in here before."

"No, first time."

"You from Lynn?"

"Nope, foreign country: Marblehead, Massachusetts."

His smile grew wider. "Different world."

"I'm investigating the Simpson murder," I said.

He reacted as if I'd just slapped him in the face.

"Don't know anything about it. Sorry, sir, I'm new." He retreated to the other end of the bar.

By eight, the place had started to fill up. I nursed the lollypop. I wanted an actual gin martini. Old habits die hard. But I switched over to soda water with lime and had a dozen raw oysters, then chatted up a half-dozen women. They all seemed to assume I was trying to pick them up. I can't say the thought didn't occur to me with a couple of them, and I even took a few numbers. But that wasn't what I'd come here for. And I was getting nowhere, anyway, half of them had no idea a murder had ever occurred, and the other half had never met the victim. Just after eleven I finally hit pay dirt.

She wasn't a kid, but she was really put together—some kind of athlete. Her shoulders and arms were feminine but incredibly toned. She moved like a gazelle—either a dancer or a gymnast for sure. Short-styled blonde hair and a classic little black dress, with the emphasis on *little*. She edged her way down the crowded bar, accompanied by a man half her age. I instantly got up and offered her my seat.

She smiled at me and took it. "I hope I'm not scaring you away," she said.

"Far from it," I said, and raised my glass. "Old school. Just can't abide a lady standing."

"A gentleman. How refreshing. Claudia Kingston," she said, and took my hand. Her eyes were the lightest blue I'd ever seen; an almost complete absence of pigment. I found myself instantly drawn to them.

"Fenway Burke," I said, and then turned to the man she'd come in with and introduced myself again.

"Robert Thornton," he said, and gave my hand far too hard a squeeze. I laughed out loud.

"Impressive, young man," I said, and then offered to buy them both a round of drinks. Claudia accepted before her escort had a chance to respond. They had martinis. I stuck with soda water and lime. She knew Nicholas Simpson all right.

"Yes, yes, he was always in here with a friend of his," she said.

"Know the guy's name?"

"Randy Rogers, a friend from school. He buys drinks for everyone."

"For you?" I asked.

"A few," she said. "He has money, but I prefer a man out of diapers." She smiled and touched my hand. I saw Robert stiffen.

"He hit the lottery or something?"

"Old money. You've heard of the Rogers Foundation?"

"Ah ... *that* Rogers. He and Nicholas get along OK?" I asked.

"Both liked to get their own way. College boys, you know." She chuckled. "All that testosterone, but they were pals."

"Right," I said. "I'll have to have a little talk with this Rogers kid."

I pulled out a picture of Shawn Corbett. "Ever see this guy in here?"

She gave me a look. "What is all this?"

"Private eye, just asking around," I said.

"Seriously?"

"Seriously."

"Oh, my God, I'm flirting with Sam Spade," she said, and then laughed.

I laughed, too. "Don't let that stop you," I said. "I'm doing a little flirting myself."

Her escort gave me a look. "She's with me," he said.

She smiled and shook her head. "Let's not be tiresome, Robert," she told him. The kid got red in the face and moved in close to me with his game face on.

I just smiled and looked him right in the eye. "Trust me, Bob, not a good idea."

He stood there for a long minute, looked to her, then back to me and excused himself, heading for the men's room.

"You're very sure of yourself, aren't you," she said.

"I am," I said.

She reached over and touched my hand again. "I like that," she said. "Is the beard new?"

"Couple of weeks."

"The gold earring's a nice touch, too."

"Live on a boat."

"Sounds romantic."

"Oh, yeah, I'm a romantic all right."

She laughed. We went back and forth. I was making more than a bit of progress.

She saw her escort coming back. Reached into her bag and pulled out her card. "Call me," she said.

I took it. "I just might." I tapped the picture of Shawn Corbett I'd left on the bar.

"Never saw him before in my life," she said.

"You sure?"

"In here? Are you kidding?"

"I see your point."

r   r   r

I CHECKED OUT THE ALLEY on my way to the car. It was plenty bright. Two floodlights did the trick. By the look of them, they'd been there forever. But I'd have to find out when they were installed. I wrote a note to myself on my pad.

CHAPTER 8

It's always best to start at the top. Dana Brown was president of The Berkeley School of Music. I was ushered into his office by a shapely young blonde. Maybe it was my imagination—I have an active one—but I'd swear we had a moment. Brown was just a few inches shorter than me and in decent shape: trim, with short dark hair just starting to recede. He was dressed in a beige summer suit with a blue and yellow bow tie. I had on my best tweeds, with patches on the elbows, no less. I could see right off the bat that I'd made a big impression. He came around from his desk and shook hands.

"You're with the Boston Police Department?"

"Formerly, I'm a private investigator." I handed him my card.

"Really. I assumed, well, so this is not an official inquiry. You're re-opening the Simpson case?"

"I'm doing some background. Randall Rogers is a student

here and a close friend of the victim. I need to speak to him and also former roommates or any students who might have information."

He took his seat and leaned back, making a steeple with his fingers. "For what purpose, Mr. Burke?"

"My client believes a man has been wrongly convicted."

Brown put his elbows on the desk. "Based on what evidence?"

"As I say, they have their beliefs. It's my job to find out if there's any substance to them."

Brown leaned back again, with just the faintest hint of a smile. "Mr. Burke, this campus was torn apart by that affair; the police, the media especially. I can't even begin to tell you."

I gave him a little smile of my own. "I'm sure it wasn't easy."

"An understatement. I have absolutely no desire to open this particular can of worms all over again."

"A man may be falsely convicted here. It's his life," I said.

"He has an extensive criminal record and is a violent man, is he not?"

"I can't argue with you there, but that has no bearing on this case."

"Do I have any legal obligation to cooperate with you?"

"No, sir, you do not, but I need some answers."

Brown shook his head. "Mr. Burke, really, you seem a decent sort. Let me be perfectly honest with you."

"Please."

"I have no desire to see any private investigator go on a fishing expedition that can only lead to nothing."

I smiled and nodded. "And?"

"And after all, the crime did not occur on campus. I do not

have the slightest intention of cooperating in any way. Have I made myself clear? Please don't make me call campus security."

"Professor, I'm beginning to get the impression you're not on my side."

"Nothing personal, Mr. Burke, I'm just doing my job."

"Of course," I said.

"I assume Rogers is a senior," I said. "Graduating in another couple of months?" Brown shook his head, not answering, then pushed his chair from his desk, leaning back. "You're not going away are you, Mr. Burke," he said.

"Nope."

He sat there for a moment not saying anything, then stood and offered me his hand. I took it. "I'm afraid this interview is over. Security will detain you if you attempt to enter the campus again."

"Oh, no, not that," I said, and then laughed. "I thank you for your time."

I got a smile out of him. "I'm sorry; I wish I could have been more helpful."

"Me too," I said as I took my leave.

I stopped a kid as I left his office. "Excuse me, could you direct me to the library?"

In the library, there was a student at the desk. Short dark hair, black lipstick and at least a dozen piercings, not counting her ears. Her arms were covered in colorful tattoos.

"Good morning," I said.

She looked up from her computer without expression. "May I help you?"

"Hope so, I need to take a look at your latest yearbook."

She went back to her screen. "They're for sale, Reference," she said. "Upstairs."

I bought a copy. His picture was more formal then most of the others. He was in a jacket and tie and not a hint of a smile. His haircut gave him that young Republican look. It seemed like he was looking at something very far away. He had quite a write-up; looked like the kid was destined for a career as a concert pianist.

The practice rooms were in the basement. They called it the dungeon and they weren't kidding. There were a dozen rooms down a long, dark, musty-smelling corridor with thick windows on each battered gray metal door. Only a couple of them were in use. Someone was really wailing on a tenor sax way down at the end. The kid had a three-day beard, a tattered Berkeley sweatshirt, loose jeans with a hole in one knee and a stocking cap pulled down tight. His eyes were closed. He rocked back and forth, really letting loose.

I knocked but he didn't hear. He had the window wide open but it made no difference. I let myself in and had an instant flashback to my wayward college days. I could have caught a buzz just standing there.

"Oh my, what is that peculiar smell?" I said.

He stopped playing instantly and just stood there looking me over, not saying a word.

"Little hospitality here?" I said.

He hesitated, then smiled, reached for a lighted jay from his music stand. After taking a hit, he offered it to me.

I followed suit. "Been a while," I said. I talked and tried to hold my breath at the same time.

He nodded and took it back, then hit it again.

"Looking for Randall Rogers. You know him?" I let the marijuana smoke out in a long exhale.

He smiled and shook his head. "Man, are you in the wrong place. He'd be over at the Annex." He handed me back the jay.

I took another hit.

"Across the street," he said, then pointed over his shoulder with his thumb.

I handed back the joint. "Thanks, man." I closed the door tight when I left. The kid got right back into it on the sax. I stopped a couple of steps down the corridor for a minute and listened. Either he'd turned me on to some really good stuff, or he was going places, because he sounded damned good.

The Annex was brand new, open and airy with a lot of glass. They told me at the front desk that Rogers was in Europe and wouldn't be back for almost three weeks. I'd have to put him on the back burner for now, but we'd be talking.

CHAPTER 9

It's never a picnic to speak with relatives of the victim, parents especially. They were high school teachers. I took the stone steps two at a time. It was a modest, red brick home on a quiet side street in Brookline. The grounds were impeccable; someone was a gardener. The door opened just as I was about to ring the bell.

She was a little woman. It would be a stretch to call her five feet tall. She had gray hair pulled back a bit too tight, wore a housedress and not a trace of makeup. Her only jewelry was her wedding ring. Her movements were bird-like. She looked up at me, then around the front yard, as if expecting someone to jump out at her.

"You're Burke."

"Mrs. Simpson?"

She didn't bother to respond, but took my arm and led me inside. "My husband's out back in his woodworking shop. He doesn't know you're here. I didn't want to upset him."

"I just have a few questions." I took out a small notepad, very official, and took a seat opposite her on the sofa. There on the coffee table was a picture of a beaming, handsome young man on a golf green. I picked it up.

"Your son?" I asked.

She nodded, tight-lipped. "Nicholas was an avid golfer," she said. She pointed to an elegant set of highly polished clubs in an alligator bag, resting in a corner. "Those were his," she said.

I'm no expert on golf clubs, but they looked more than just pricey. Far beyond the reach of the middle class—custom-made for sure.

"They're magnificent," I said, getting up. "Mind if I have a closer look at them?"

She nodded.

I took out a wood, perfectly balanced with a titanium shaft. There was a logo stamped into the handle: "Chas McGowen, Saint Andrews, since 1821, The choice of champions." The bag gleamed alligator. "Must have cost a fortune," I said.

"A gift from a friend. All the way from Scotland." she said.

"Nicholas played in Scotland?"

"Oh yes, several times," she said, and then gave me a look. "Officer Burke, I can't imagine what else I can tell you that we haven't already told the Lynn Police."

"I'm not with the Lynn—"

"Boston?"

"I'm a private investigator, Mrs. Simpson."

She gave me a level stare. "Private?"

"I work for the defendant."

She stiffened. The skin on her forehead drew tight.

"You're trying to get him off." Her voice rose. "After all this time, you're trying to get him off!" She was screaming now.

There was a commotion out back and her husband came rushing in. He was a trim man, not much taller than his wife, with a pencil mustache, heavy-soled shoes and a tan, working man's uniform. He had sawdust in his thinning, salt-and-pepper hair.

"Melissa, what's—" He saw me and stood stock-still.

"He's a private investigator, Herbert, trying to get that filthy animal off." Her voice cracked. She'd developed a slight tremor, almost like a palsy.

He stood there, not saying a word.

"I'm looking for the truth, Mr. Simpson, wherever it leads."

Simpson ignored me and took his wife in his arms. She leaned into him. "We thought this was over with," he said.

I nodded. "I'm sorry." There was a picture on the wall, a bright young man, smiling, with a violin. "Your son was a musician?"

"Berkeley School of Music," Mr. Simpson said. "He was a senior when ... "

"Randall Rogers, did you know him?"

"Roommates their freshman year." Mr. Simpson said. "I don't see—"

"Close?"

She pulled away from her husband. "Yes, Mr. Burke, congratulations. Our son was gay. Will that help you set his murderer free?"

"Mrs. Simpson—"

"Get out," she said. "Get out and never come back. Do you understand?"

Mr. Simpson put his arm on her shoulder. "Don't make me call the police," he added.

"Mr. Simpson, I'm sorry for your trouble." Well, that was productive, I found out the kid was gay and a golfer. I'd have to make a note when I spoke to Shawn, *The Animal,* Corbett's parents to get the name of the country club he belonged to. I let myself out.

CHAPTER 10

Shawn Corbett's mother, Katharine Corbett, had to be in her late fifties. I knocked and instantly got a "Just a minute!" from behind the door of her Dorchester third-floor walk-up. She was tall and slender with short blonde hair and wore a gray pinstriped suit. Not at all what I'd expected, and quite attractive. She took my hand.

"Fenway Burke," I said.

"I'm Katharine. Tiny told me to expect you." She stepped aside to let me in. There was a pot of coffee on the stove. She poured me a cup, and we sat down at the kitchen table. She looked at her watch.

"You have some place to go?"

"I work at a bank," she said. "Assistant manager, but I told them I'd be late. How can I help you?" She looked me right in the eye.

I pulled out my pad. "Little background," I said. "And some

follow-up. There's the matter of the late-model Lincoln. Do you know of any friend who might have loaned it to him?"

She frowned and shook her head. "No one. Michael O'Brian's the only boy I know with a car. But it's no Lincoln, and it's a wreck. It must be at least ten years old."

I wrote down the name. "He a close friend?"

She nodded.

"How can I get hold of him?"

She got up. "I have the number," she said. "He lives with his mother, right around the corner."

"Shawn a member of any gang that you know of?"

She shook her head, but there was the slightest twitch on the corner of her lips. "No, just the kids in the neighborhood." She lowered her eyes and spoke to her hands. "My son's not a criminal, Mr. Burke. It's the drugs; the drugs got him." She took a deep breath. "I feel so powerless."

Neither one of us said anything for a minute.

"Okay if I take a look in his room?"

She nodded and stood up. "He got his own apartment just before they arrested him, but I still kept it for him. I always hoped he'd be back." Her voice cracked.

She stood in the doorway as I went through his things. There was a single bed and a battered dresser. The walls were covered with posters, from Star Wars to Big Popi, David Ortiz, of the Red Sox, a half-naked Christina Aguilera. There were a couple of dozen video games and an over-sized TV that took up half the room. Shawn had a lot going on. If I hadn't known better, I'd have figured a twelve-year-old lived there.

I looked to Katharine.

"It would have been different if he'd had a man around growing up," she said. "I did the best I could, but ... "

"Divorced?" I asked.

She didn't look me in the eye. "Something like that."

"Rough world out there."

"Do you think you can do anything for him?"

"That's what I'm trying to find out."

I put her through it. All the questions the cops had already asked her a thousand times when they'd shown up with the search warrant. Could she give me all his known associates? Where had he been the night of the murder? What did he do for work and on and on and on, and then into it all over again. She was a trooper, but ended up calling in sick at the bank. Going over all this again really took it out of her.

Michael O'Brian got the same treatment—no surprises. Shawn Corbett was a crack-head and a loner. What he was doing in Lynn, and how he got there in the first place was a complete mystery.

CHAPTER 11

"Ahoy!"

"Megan!"

I waved from my deck chair. It was a little after six.

"Just in time for the early-bird special, come aboard."

"I brought a friend. I hope that's okay." She pulled the leash of a good-sized jet black Portuguese Water Dog as she came up the ramp to the deck of the *Queen Anne's Revenge*. She wore loose-fitting khakis with a pink polo jersey and boat shoes.

"Glad you did. The kids will be delighted. "What's his name?"

"Spot."

"But he's all black."

"I always wanted a dog named Spot."

"A dream come true." Rowlf and Blanche came up out of the hold, tails wagging.

I gave Megan a light kiss on the cheek. "Glass of wine?"

She smiled. "Fine."

"I steamed lobsters and then put them on ice. Ought to be fine in about a half-hour," I said. "Chilled Monkey Bay, Sauvignon Blanc. Sound okay?"

"You're sweeping me off my feet."

"That's the idea."

Our dogs got acquainted. It was the usual routine: butt-sniffing and then settling in. I had a couple of deck chairs set up with a small redwood table. An opened bottle of wine protruded from a silver wine bucket on a stand beside the table. I freshened my oversized, long-stemmed wine glass and filled hers halfway to the top, draining the bottle.

"I'd better get another one of these from below deck."

"Good plan. You didn't have to get dressed up for me, you know."

I was barefoot in cut-offs with a red short-sleeved jersey that was a little frayed around the collar. "Didn't want to take unfair advantage. After all, it is our first date, and I'm quite a package."

"I can see that." She took a chair as I went below for another bottle.

It was a perfect night, with just a hint of a breeze. Marblehead Harbor is like something out of a travel book. Sailboats bobbed gently on their moorings as other boats came in from either a fun day excursion or a day hauling lobster traps.

The sound of laughter and good conversation drifted across the water. The Harbor boasted over three hundred craft, a mix of pleasure and working boats. We sipped our wine and did the chilled lobster thing with cocktail sauce as we watched the show and got to know each other. She had all kinds of questions. I told her about my hitch in the Special Forces, being an instructor on hand-to-hand combat, my aborted career as a cop, getting shot in the hip and opting for early retirement and, finally, going out on my own. She laughed when I told her I'd never done well with authority figures anyway.

"And that's how you became a private eye?"

"'Bout the size of it," I said; then I brought her up to speed on Shawn Corbett.

"If I can help you with anything else, let me know," she said.

"Can't stand the idea of losing one, huh?"

She laughed. "Are you kidding? I'm a public defender; I lose nine hundred ninety-nine out of a thousand."

"No picnic on my end either, knocking on a lot of doors with not much to show for it at the moment."

She nodded and didn't say anything for a second, then leaned her chair back on two legs. "So this is it, *tu casa*."

"Yep," I said. "My home."

"Lucky you," she said. "You're divorced, I assume."

I nodded. "Took forever, just became final a couple of months ago. You too?"

"Separated," she said.

"Ah, long way to go, but you're following through?"

"Have to."

I gave her a smile. "A real bastard, huh?"

"He's kind, sweet, gentle and accomplished, a surgeon at Mass General. Good-looking, too. His parents were missionaries."

"Missionaries?"

She smiled. "I wouldn't kid you."

"Sounds like a bad one, all right."

She laughed. "We've just grown apart. I met him at a dance when he was in medical school."

"When you were a law student?"

"Right. I never could stand the sight of blood."

"Might have been better off in medical school," I said.

"Now you sound like my father."

"And you work as a public defender to give something back?"

"You could say that. I'm a trust fund kid."

I nodded. "Harvard?"

"Yes, as a matter of fact. You?"

"You're talking to a dropout from North Shore Community College. My ex went to Harvard."

"Really, what's her name?"

"Evelyn Lowell."

She laughed out loud. "My God, Evie Lowell."

"You know her?"

"Know of her, the deb. Her family must have really loved you."

"I received mixed reviews."

"I'll bet."

The dogs began to stir. "'Bout time we took our charges for a walk," I said, standing.

We got the leashes and took them down the walkway onto Front Street, plastic bags in hand. Mine was considerably larger than hers. The dogs did their business quickly and we did our follow-up, depositing our bags in a trash basket.

"The joys of parenthood," I said.

She smiled and looked up at the transom of my boat. "The *Queen Anne's Revenge*. It just dawned on me; that was Blackbeard the pirate's ship, wasn't it?"

"A pure coincidence."

"I'm not so sure." She took my hand.

"You up for a moonlight sail?" I asked.

"Hard to say no."

Poor Megan; she fell victim to the vaunted Burke charm, a force for which there is no known defense. She ended up staying over.

CHAPTER 12

The sun was just coming up in beautiful South Boston. All three eyewitnesses had disconnected phones with no new number listed. It was time to start knocking on doors. Both Sullivan and O'Shea had moved out and left no forwarding address. Just one more to go, at twenty-one K Street: the delightful abode of one Peter Mahoney. It was a crumbling three-decker with a rusted chain-link fence, no grass, and trash scattered everywhere. I was just making my way up the steps to the front door when I was blindsided by a spotted pit bull that came out of nowhere, snarling and growling as he lunged for my leg. I pulled away just in time as he came up short, straining at his heavy chain. My heart skipped a beat.

I heard footsteps coming down the stairs. The guy was raising hell, screaming obscenities. The door swung open and I got my first look. He was barefoot, a little guy with rheumy eyes and a gut hanging over a pair of faded blue work pants that looked like hand-me-downs from the Roosevelt administration. His T-shirt was filthy and threadbare and torn around the collar. There was whiskey on his breath. He looked me up and down.

"What the fuck do you want?" he said.

I was still a bit shaken by my near miss with the dog.

"Well?" he said.

"Peter Mahoney," I said. "That you?"

He made a face and started to close the door on me. I grabbed it.

"Owe the guy some money," I said.

He hesitated for a second. "Yeah? Son of a bitch skipped out on three months' rent."

"Might be able to help you out with that," I said. "You got any idea how I can get hold of him?"

"He ain't the kind of guy leaves no forwarding address," he said.

"A hangout, maybe?"

He stood there staring at me. I looked him right in the eyes. I didn't see any light in them.

"Kelly's," he finally said.

"The pub?"

"Fuck, you think? He ain't there, he's in some other gin mill. That's where he spends his rent money."

I nodded. "Appreciate it," I said. "Do what I can to get your money."

He made a face. "Yeah, right."

Piece of cake, I thought; *can't be more that fifty thousand pubs in Southie.* Long day ahead. I'd make the rounds; with any luck I'd find all of the witnesses. One day turned into two, then three. It took me the better part of the week to catch up with Mr. Mahoney.

I was about to call it quits for the day, but there it was, on my left as I was driving by: the L Street Tavern. What the hell, I'd make it my last stop. The L had gotten a real shot in the arm there for a while, having been featured in *Good Will Hunting*. The owners jazzed the joint up with their newfound wealth, thinking it would go on forever. It didn't; the novelty wore off in less than a year, and though Southie was in the process of gentrification in spots, the L was not one of those spots. It was a big improvement though. Now, when one of the patrons pissed his pants, he did so on a plush leather barstool.

I got some looks coming in. Might not have been a great plan to wear my lavender Polo jersey, but it was a beautiful day and comfort is important in my line of work—critical, in my case. I'm sure the patrons thought my multi-pocket chinos and boat shoes were a nice touch, too. I took a seat at the bar and ordered a Guinness. A guy has to fit in. The bartender was a couple inches taller than I am, with shaved head and milk-white skin. He put a pint in front of me.

"Looking for a guy named Peter Mahoney. You know him?"

"This is your lucky day, pal." He turned and nodded to a patron down at the very end of the bar working on a shot and a beer. "There's your man."

I thanked him and moved on over, taking the stool next to Mahoney. He was about twenty-five with buzz-cut blonde hair and a bad complexion. He was in jeans that had been none-too-neatly cut off just above the knees. His wife-beater T-shirt had seen better days. No socks and his sneakers in the same condition as the wife-beater. He had an Irish flag tattooed on his upper arm. There was no smoking in the bar, a new Massachusetts law, but I could smell cigarettes on him.

He looked over at me as I sat down.

"You Peter Mahoney?"

He didn't respond. He looked right at me, but his eyes were glassy.

"Peter Mahoney, you him?"

He tossed back what was left of his shot. "You a cop? You don't look like no cop." He sounded like he'd just come over on the boat that morning.

"I'm no cop."

"Gay, then, fuck off."

I gave him my very best hard-guy stare. "I'm a private investigator, looking into the Simpson murder. Name's Fenway Burke."

"He snorted. "Fenway," he said.

"That's right. You got something against the Sox?"

He just sat there. I offered my hand. He ignored it.

"What part of 'fuck off' didn't you understand?" he said.

I smiled and grabbed his wrist, giving it a little twist. There's two ways to do it. One goes against the natural way to bend it; enough pressure, it'll snap like a bread stick. I can apply more than enough pressure. You twist it the other way, with the natural bend, it'll hurt like hell for a moment but be perfectly fine once you let go. I went for option number two.

"Jesus."

I held on tight. "Don't fuck with me. Answer my questions and I'll buy you a few drinks, no big thing, okay?"

"Okay, okay, just let go, for Christ's sake."

I did. He looked at me and rubbed his wrist. Guy had no intention of screwing with me. I motioned to the bartender. "Couple more over here, whatever he's drinking."

Mahoney threw down his shot right off the bat and took a big sip of beer.

"Keep 'em coming," I said to the bartender. "So, Mr. Mahoney, you saw Shawn Corbett shoot Simpson."

"That's right."

"Tell me exactly what happened."

"Heard some yellin'; went around the corner to see; and there it was. Guy had a gun on him. His hands were up. Next thing, bang, bang, bang and it was over."

"Just like that?"

"Just like that."

"Weren't you afraid?"

"Course I was afraid."

"What'd you do?"

"Hid behind the building and hoped to Jesus he didn't see me."

"What then?"

"Saw him drive off in a gray Lincoln."

I nodded. "There were two other witnesses. O'Shea and Sullivan. Did you know them?"

"No, never even saw them."

"What were you doing in Lynn in the first place?"

"Out on the town, having a good time."

"You go there a lot?"

"That's right."

"Name two bars you go to," I said.

No response.

"One, then."

"I haven't been back since the shooting," Mahoney said.

"You've never been there in your life," I said, and grabbed his shoulder.

He looked down at the bar. "I been there," he said.

"You're lying. Who put you up to it?"

He got to his feet. "I don't got to talk to you."

I grabbed him and put him back down. "Oh, but you do," I said. "Might as well come clean. I'll be talking to Sullivan and O'Shea."

He threw back his shot. "You ain't talking to O'Shea. He's dead."

"Thought you didn't know him." I could almost hear the gears turning in his head. They were moving slowly, but they were moving. He had a blank look, and then finally came to life.

"Ya hear things. You know how it is," he said.

"Uh-huh. Where do you work?"

"I got nothin' to say." He got up again. I forced him back down a second time.

"Hey, take it easy," he said, fidgeting in his seat.

I backed off, and just pressed him for general information. I knew he was lying and he knew I knew. For now that was okay.

"You got a job?"

"Off and on, forklift operator when they need me, down at Boston Metals."

I took out my note pad. "Southie?"

"Yeah."

"You're not on K Street anymore. What's your current address?"

"Four-thirty-one Elm."

"How long?"

"Coupla months"

"Lets see some ID," I said.

"Huh?"

"Your license. I need to confirm your address."

He hesitated for a second, and then handed it over. Sure enough: four-thirty-one Elm. At least he wasn't lying about that. If his ID was a fake, it was damned good.

"Father?" I said.

"Dead?"

"Mother?" And on and on, the standard investigative routine but he refused to give me anything more. I left him more than half in the bag. I planned to do a little checking up on my new pal, Mr. Mahoney.

I ran a criminal background check on him over the Internet: not a single felony— all misdemeanors in this country—but he had done time in Ireland. He never would have gotten into the country if his father hadn't been born here. The kid was a known member of the IRA. Could have knocked me over with a feather when I read that; Mahoney didn't strike me as a patriot.

O'Shea was dead, shot in the head while fleeing the scene of a robbery. Mark Sullivan had fallen off the face of the earth. I had his mug shot from a minor bust and showed it around. Seemed he'd just about lived in the Erie Pub, then suddenly stopped showing up. I'd have Tiny's boys keep an eye out for him; maybe he'd place a bet somewhere, but my gut told me Sullivan had skipped town. I'd managed to get his Social Security number. There's an Internet agency I subscribe to, Credit Aware; if he opened a bank account or applied for a credit card, I'd have him. I figured it was a long shot, but at the moment I didn't have a whole lot of options.

My cell chirped. It was the big man, said he had some inside information on Corbett and put the emphasis on *inside*. I was to meet a Mr. Patty Doyle. We'd have lunch the very next day.

CHAPTER 13

Tiny ordered his second beer at the Landing, right down the street from Maddie's. Despite Tiny's ribbing, I stuck with soda water and lime. We had the place to ourselves; all of the other patrons were out on the back deck, right on the water, watching the boat traffic and working on drinks with umbrellas in them.

The only view we had was of Sharon, who pulled our drinks and took care of the waitresses at the service bar. She'd just graduated from Salem State and was looking for work as a gym teacher. Her long brown hair was pulled back. Her dress was modest enough, but form-fitting and hard to miss. She tended to get a lot of tips. After placing Tiny's beer in front of him, she smiled and looked him right in the eye. I wasn't there at all, apparently.

"Would you like something to eat, Danny?" she said, touching his hand.

He smiled back at her. "I've been thinking about that. Maybe in a while."

She nodded. "I'm here when you're ready." She went back to the service bar as a waitress approached.

Note to self: never to sit next to Tiny again. Across, that was the way to go. Sitting side-by-side with Tiny made me look like some kind of runt.

Tiny watched her walk away. She had a major league J Lo thing going on.

I brought him back. "Hey," I said, looking at my watch. "Where the hell's Patty Doyle?"

Doyle used to work as one of Tiny's collectors, and had spent the last three years at Cedar Junction. He knew Corbett from the old neighborhood and shared a cell with him for a close to a year. Doyle was a tough guy with freckles and red hair, and he was quick to take offense.

"He'll be here all right," said Tiny. "Just got out the day before yesterday."

Right on cue, Doyle walked through the door. Tiny got up, shook hands, introduced us and bought another round. They caught up for a while. Tiny offered him back his old job. Then it was my turn.

"You close to Corbett on the inside?" I said.

Doyle made a face. "Known him since I was a kid. What about it?"

"Just checking out his story," I said. "You were cellmates?"

"Yeah."

"He ever talk about the Simpson case?"

Doyle snorted. "Never talked about nothing else, guy don't know nothing."

I took another sip of soda. "You shared a cell with him for a year, and he never admitted anything, not even a hint?" I said.

"Nothing," Doyle confirmed. "Nothing at all."

I ended up buying lunch. Doyle hit me up for the twin lobster special and drank a gallon of beer. I stuck with soda water and then came at him a dozen ways, but it always wound up the same. If Corbett did know anything about the murder, he sure as hell was doing a fine job of keeping his mouth shut. Doyle took off around two-thirty.

"That was productive, huh?" Tiny said.

"Corbett's story's consistent. Things just might heat up," I said.

"You figure someone might put the arm on ya?"

"Mahoney's story's bunk and someone's got something to hide. I'm making waves, so yeah. I figure there's a pretty damn good chance."

"You plan to keep nosing around?"

"You paid me, didn't you?" I said. "Anyway, this thing's actually getting interesting. You got my back?"

"I got your back."

It slowed down at the service bar. Sharon came back over, though Tiny's beer wasn't even half-gone.

"I get off at five, if you're still in town," she said to Tiny. "If not ..." She handed him a slip of paper with her number on it. Two more waitresses came back with drink orders. She smiled and went back to work.

I turned to Tiny. "If you read between the lines, you may be on the right track with her."

"Ya think?"

"Wouldn't steer you wrong, I'm a lady's man," I said.

"Right, and I'm a very handsome man with my wallet on." Tiny polished off the last of his beer and left a hundred-dollar bill for a tip.

Within a half-hour after lunch, he called on my cell and told me to expect Ax and a half-dozen of his crew to show up. Ax was Tiny's number-two man, a genuine misfit, bounced out of the SEALs for beating the hell out of a superior officer. He was a field-certified expert in at least a dozen weapons and a bona fide maniac in hand-to-hand combat. Nobody fooled with Ax.

They were renting a house on State Street, right across from Maddie's. I had already turned on my surveillance system on the boat: remote cameras, motion detectors, the whole deal. I'd had it installed a couple of years back when I was still working divorce cases. An errant husband caught in the act with his girlfriend had made ugly threats against me, then skipped town after I had the gear set up. This was the first time I'd turned it on.

If anybody did come around trying to stop my nosing around the Corbett thing, at least I'd see them coming.

CHAPTER 14

Megan was sitting on a deck chair, waiting on me to come up with a chilled bottle and a couple of glasses. She was scratching behind Rowlf's ears. Blanche and Spot were stretched out on the deck. Megan smiled when I appeared, wine bucket in hand.

"You think we'll need the bucket? Usually polish it off before it has a chance to get warm," I said.

"It might be nice to act like civilized people for once," she said.

"What's that got to do with me?"

"More with me, I think."

She suddenly went stiff and took my hand. A menacing man who was built like a brick with a Mohawk haircut approached the boat. His arms were the size of most men's legs. Spot growled. Rowlf and Blanche ignored him.

"How you doing, Fenway?"

"Just fine."

He nodded without a word and left without acknowledging Megan in any way.

She watched him walk off, still holding my hand. "One of your friends from Maddie's?"

"An associate."

"You mean you work with him?"

"Works for Tiny. You met Tiny."

"The big man at the gym, hard to forget," she said.

"He does tend to stand out in a crowd."

She finally let go of my hand. "And what does he do, your associate?"

"Odd jobs. Breaking heads mostly. His name's Ax."

She gave me a look.

"I'm not sure if that's his Christian name, but he's going to be around for a while, just taking precautions."

"What?"

"It's the Corbett thing. If there is a cover up, likely someone's getting nervous."

"My God, is it safe?"

I thought she was going to run for her life. I laughed. "Oh, it's safe all right. Tiny's staying with me. Ax and his boys are right around the corner.

"This is like something out of a movie." She was thoughtful for a moment. "You're carrying a gun, aren't you? I mean right now, as we're having a glass of wine."

"Yeah, but just a little one." I reached behind my back and pulled my twenty-five caliber Beretta from its holster under my jersey. I put it on the table.

"A little one."

"Yes, well, you know—it's the weekend," I said.

She drained her glass in one big gulp and then held it up for a refill. I'd never seen her do that before. I filled it up, right to the brim.

"You, Mr. Burke, are like no other man in my experience."

"Not sure if that's good or bad."

"I'm not either."

CHAPTER 15

Tiny and I were below deck, working on our second cup of take-out coffee. I had him halfway hooked on Starbucks. He refused to switch over from the Dunkin' Donuts donuts, though; I'd need a little time on that end. Starbucks' pastry is a much tougher sell.

"You got in late last night," I said.

Tiny talked with his mouth full. "Coupla cocktails with Sharon. She didn't get off 'til midnight."

"And you got in at six. Things seem to be progressing," I said.

Tiny grabbed another donut and stuffed the entire thing in his mouth. He answered me like a guy at the dentist. "Gentlemen never talk about such things, but yeah."

"I see."

"How you making out with Megan?"

"Ax spooked her."

"He does have that tendency. Good guy, though," Tiny said.

"I'll let her know. I'm sure it'll make all the difference."

"She's not just another one of your bimbos, is she?"

"Something special about her."

"Special? You've known her what … a half-hour or something?"

"What can I tell ya."

Tiny shook his head and grabbed yet another donut; his cell phone chirped. He held up a finger while answering. "Yeah … yeah." He hung up. "We got company."

I looked at my watch—just after eleven. "Getting a late start, how many?"

"Five."

"Guess they figure there's strength in numbers."

"So do I."

I heard them coming on deck, and the dogs reacted. The footsteps stopped abruptly.

"So much for the element of surprise," I said, then yelled at the hatch. "It's okay, boys, they won't bite. Come on down!" They came down the steep steps like a ladder, one-by-one, their backs to us— land lubbers. They were good-sized guys, all in white windbreakers and jeans. The first one down was at least my height with a shaved head and sunglasses. They raised their hands as they turned around. Tiny had two, forty-four magnum pistols trained on them. I had my puny little nine millimeter Glock.

"Morning, fellas," I said.

I disarmed all five while Tiny kept them covered. There was a commotion on deck. Once again the dogs reacted. I calmed them down. Ax stuck his head through the hatch.

"You guys okay down there?"

"Never better," Tiny said. "Get yourselves a cup of coffee."

Ax smiled and did just that.

"So," I said. "Do you gentlemen have an appointment?"

Skinhead kept his cool. "You Burke?"

I turned to Tiny. "Guy's not as dumb as he looks," I said.

"I'll take book on that," Tiny said.

"What can I do for you?"

"Got something to tell you," he said, his hands still held high.

"I'm listening," I said.

"You're on that Corbett thing."

"And?"

"Man don't like it, leave the motherfucker alone."

"Which man?"

"I said what I got to say," Skinhead informed me.

I smiled at Tiny, then turned to Skinhead. "You're not talking?"

"You got ears, motherfucker?"

I used the Glock like a hammer on his noggin. Skinhead hit the floor. Blood ran down his face. I helped him up on his unsteady legs and slammed him against the wall.

"You've seen one end of this thing," I said, with the Glock jammed under his chin. "I can show you the other if you like. Who sent you?"

Nothing.

I jammed the pistol in harder. "Who sent you?"

Nothing.

"Who sent you?" I said again.

Still nothing. The guy surprised me.

"Screw it." I let Skinhead go. "Okay, now make tracks."

One of the others spoke up for the first time. "Our guns?"

"You got to be kidding me," Tiny said. "Get the fuck out of here."

"And have a nice day," I said.

They scampered up the steps, giving Skinhead a helping hand.

"They expected to find you alone," Tiny said.

"Glad I wasn't." I called Ax on my cell. "Put a tail on them and make sure they don't know they're being followed." Ax grunted a response and hung up.

"No need to insult the man," Tiny said.

I shrugged and put my cell back in my pocket. "You know me, just making sure."

Ax got back to me in less than a half-hour. Our visitors made a straight line to the Lynn, Massachusetts, offices of one Steven Washington.

"You know this guy, Tiny?"

"Stevie Washington, I know him." Tiny said.

CHAPTER 16

Tiny filled me in on Stevie Washington. He was a small-time North Shore book who'd laid some bets off on Tiny from time to time when the action got a little too heavy for him. Tiny thought he was also involved in dope and loan sharking. Penny ante though, all of his operations confined to Lynn, Revere and a piece of Everett. His big claim to fame was majority ownership in the Lynn Bowl-A-Rama, strictly a low-rent kind of guy.

"Make a call on the guy if you like," Tiny said.

"Nah, this one I'll handle on my own," I said. With Tiny and his boys, things sometimes had a way of getting out of hand.

I pulled him up on the on the Internet. About what I expected: a half-dozen arrests over the years for taking book. He'd done a couple of years at Walpole in the early nineties on a plea bargain for strong arm, part of the loan sharking thing. Nothing after that.

STEVIE'S OFFICE WAS ON Western Ave. in Lynn, a place of business befitting his position in the community: a crumbling three-decker right across from the General Electric plant. He had his offices, such as they were, on the first floor, lived on the second and rented out the third; a real American success story. There was a spanking new Cadillac CTS in the driveway, looking out of place. Tiny had picked me up a nondescript gray Ford Taurus. I parked across the street and waited, just before three. I didn't have to wait long. I knew Stevie from his mug shot. Skinhead walked him to his car. Stevie was very slight, and moved with an easy, fluid motion. He had unruly sparse wisps of hair on top with a ring of thick jet-black hair on the sides and light chin whiskers like a jazz man. He wore a lightweight sport coat without a tie. Skinhead waved good-bye, and I fell in behind Stevie's car, making sure he didn't spot my tail.

We arrived at the Lynn Bowl-A-Rama in less than ten minutes. He parked illegally out front. I watched him go in and then headed down the street a couple of blocks and found an open meter. I took a hike back, went to the counter, got a lane and rented shoes. It was New England *candle pin* bowling, found nowhere else in the country. I hadn't been bowling since I was in high school. I took my alley. Stevie was nowhere in sight. I threw three balls with mixed results and then saw Stevie coming out of his office. He was in an untucked, blue and white bowling shirt, and he waved to a half-dozen other guys in the same getup, a couple of lanes down from me. A bar waitress in a short skirt took orders as Stevie grabbed a seat and picked up the first round.

A half-dozen other players came in wearing red bowling shirts with the logo, "Big A Auto Parts," on the back. They took the lane right next to Stevie and company. There were catcalls back and forth, and then the action began—league play. I was in for the wide world of sports. I kept an eye on them, nursed a coke and bowled two complete strings, taking my time, then finally went to the bar and grabbed a sandwich as the action continued.

Big night for Stevie; he had the most strikes and bought most of the drinks, a real high roller. They finally wrapped it up just after seven. Stevie tipped the waitress, grabbed her ass and headed for the door, still in his bowling shirt.

I came up behind him in the parking lot as he was opening his car door. Reaching out, I spun him around.

He turned, red in the face. "What the fuck!"

"We need to talk," I said.

"You crazy or somethin'?" He reached back under his shirt. I grabbed his arm and then nailed him with a short right to the point of his jaw. He went down hard, and broke into a sweat. I patted him down and pulled a vintage 1911A forty-five from a holster in the small of his back. He struggled to get up, using the car for support as I held his own pistol on him. I racked the slide and watched him get to his feet in stages.

"Nice piece. Haven't seen one of these in a while. You steal it from Sergeant York?" I asked.

"What the fuck you want?" There was blood coming from the corner of his mouth.

"Like I said. We have to talk."

"What! ... What?" He had tossed back a lot of beer. He leaned against the caddy and tried to catch his breath.

"There, now isn't that better?" I said.

"Tough guy."

"That'd be me."

"So?"

"You sent your boys to rough me up," I said.

There was a flash of recognition. "Oh, man, I didn't know you was wit' the big man. Ain't lookin' for no trouble."

"Who sent you?" I said.

"Guy I a owe a favor," Stevie said.

"Cop?"

Stevie looked down at his feet. "Yeah," he said.

"You paying off?" I said.

"Who ain't?"

"Quinn, I assume."

Stevie said nothing.

"You got a name?" I said.

"I can't rat on no cop."

I thought about it for a moment. I already knew.

"All he wanted me to do was rough you up; ain't no killer."

"I got that much figured out. You try roughing me up again, I'll let Tiny know. He's not as kindhearted as I am."

Stevie held up his hands. "Yeah, yeah, yeah, anything you say. I'm sorry, man, real sorry."

"That, my friend, is painfully obvious." I unloaded his forty-five and tossed it on the pavement, then took my leave. I wasn't worried about him picking it up.

I called the Lynn Police Department on my cell and got voicemail. Officer Charles Quinn was away on personal business, to return by the end of the week. I didn't bother leaving word, as I had a feeling I'd be hearing from him soon enough. I got his address from an old contact of mine. Monument Ave., Swampscott—right on the ocean. Damn pricey for a cop. The Town Hall showed the home had been purchased just three months after Shawn Corbett's conviction.

CHAPTER 17

I was working the computer in my office when someone knocked on the door. My old pal Skinhead and three of his pals. I stood up and came around the front of my desk.

"You ain't gonna be so tough without the big man, are ya?" Skin Head said.

"Caught me alone, must be your lucky day," I said. "Thought Washington called you punks off."

"We ain't here for Washington."

"Then who are you here for?"

"None of your fucking business."

"Okay, fine. ... Quinn got something else he wants to lay on me, or is it the same old song?"

"Money in it for ya, if ya nose out," Skinhead said.

"And if I don't?"

Skinhead smiled. "I was hoping for that one."

He tried to jab my chest with his finger. I grabbed his wrist and gave it a sharp twist. I could hear it snap as he screamed and went to one knee, holding his wrist up.

I took out number two with a hard kick to the knee, bending it back in the wrong direction. He cried out and went down, writhing.

I pulled my pistol and put it right in the faces of the two men left standing. The whole thing took less than three seconds.

"You punks know the drill. Hands up." I disarmed them both and then did the same with the two on the floor.

"Now get the fuck out of here, before ya piss me off," I said.

Neither one of them said a word. They just helped the other two up and headed out the door. I could hear them trying to help the guy with the bad knee down the stairs.

"Jesus, take it easy, will ya?"

I leaned back against my desk; so much for the tough guys.

I called Quinn on my cell. He answered on the first ring.

"Your boys just left," I said.

"Who is this?" Quinn said.

"Cut the shit," I said.

"I know you sent them after me."

"Prove it."

"Not my job, but I figure there'll be an investigation."

"There's nothing to tie me to anything," Quinn said. "Just a lot of noise."

"Maybe. Nice house you bought."

"Got nothing to do with anything. You think I'm stupid?"

"I think you got a problem, no matter how well you think you've got your tracks covered."

Silence on his end.

"You set Corbett up."

He said nothing.

"Question is, who paid you and why?"

Still nothing.

"You got anybody else going to pay me a visit?"

"You'll kill us both. I'm telling ya, man-to-man, stay the fuck out."

"Can't do that," I said. "On the job."

"You lay off, they'll make it worth your while," Quinn said. "Trust me on that one."

"I don't see that happening," I said.

"Stupid," Quinn said.

"You come clean now, it'll go a whole lot easier on you," I said.

The phone went dead.

CHAPTER 18

It was time to do my follow-up with Peter Mahoney. He was expecting me. The hallway was beyond tired: faded wallpaper peeling here and there and wood trim badly in need of fresh paint. I made my way up the stairs to Margaret Mahoney's third-floor apartment. I had on my tweed sportcoat and tie and looked at least halfway official. She opened the door on the third knock; a pretty woman with styled gray hair and light blue eyes. Her housedress was clean and pressed, but frayed around the sleeves.

"Peter," she said. "I'm sorry, he's not here."

"Better if he kept our appointment," I said. "No point in running away. Mind if I ask you a few questions. It's about the Simpson murder. Peter was a witness."

She frowned, but then stepped back and let me in. The furnishings were from the fifties, but the place was neat and clean.

"I don't know why you'd want to speak to me. I know nothing

about it."

"Just routine—background information on Peter."

She gave me a look.

I smiled. "He's got nothing to fear from me, Mrs. Mahoney. This is all just routine."

She nodded quickly and offered me tea. It was the last thing I wanted but I took her up on it. We sat at the table in the kitchen. I spent close to a half-hour with her. She didn't tell me anything I didn't already know.

"He's not in any trouble then?" she said.

"No—as I say—just background."

"He's a good boy, but I worry."

"Easy to get in with the wrong crowd."

She took a sip of tea. "There's that, and the trouble with his uncle."

"In Ireland? He's the IRA connection?" I said.

She looked at me for a moment, not responding, then nodded. "Back in Ireland, yes."

"Has he been active here in the States with them?" I said.

She made a face. "He's done security work for them, at fundraisers. I don't know what else, but when he gets a call he drops everything."

"I thought he left that all behind him."

"It never ends, Mr. Burke. My brother, he was in and out of British prisons all his life. He was a god to Peter."

"I see."

"I just don't want him getting mixed up in anything. That's why we came to America in the first place."

"Ireland's a long way away."

"Not so far as you might think." She poured me another cup of tea.

I thought about what she said for a moment, and then touched her gently on the shoulder. I gave her my card.

"If there's ever anything I can do, give me a call." I don't know what made me say it. Somehow I just thought it was something she needed to hear.

CHAPTER 19

Tiny had a pitcher of beer all to himself at Maddie's bar. I stuck with my soda water, on the clock and with the boss to boot. Whiff was absent. I figured he was either at a funeral or getting married. I filled Tiny in about the punks dropping by and my visit to Mrs. Mahoney.

"Jesus Christ," Tiny said. The animal was actually telling the truth."

"You just figuring that out?" I said. "All I have to do is find out who's behind it." Tiny slapped me on the back. "Oh, is that all," he said. "But what's all this IRA bullshit?"

"Probably nothing, but you asked what I'm up to, so I'm telling you."

"If the IRA's involved in this, then I'm Boy George." Tiny said.

I laughed. "Not what you'd call the most likely scenario, but I follow up on everything; Basic Detective Work 101. Can't see our boy in anything political, but who knows? He might have stumbled into something and didn't even know it. Anyway, at this point I can't rule anything out. We'll just have to see what unfolds."

"Yeah, right." Tiny said.

I shook my head. "I'm trying to get hold of this Randal Rogers and track down the other witness. He's next on my list. Mahoney knew what he was talking about. O'Shea's dead."

"IRA get him, did they?"

"Armed robbery; off-duty cop shot him in the head in the parking lot of a 7-Eleven."

"He was the perp?"

"Nearly two hundred bucks on him when he bought it," I said.

"Ah ... big time."

"Yeah. No leads at all on Sullivan. Witness number two's vanished off the face of the earth."

"Wonderful," Tiny said.

We both turned as the door opened, expecting to see Whiff. It wasn't him. The new arrival was a big guy, heavy through the chest and shoulders and at least my height, with dark brown hair and a Boston Red Sox cap pulled down over his forehead. He had a full beard, well-trimmed and long, and a ponytail. He reminded me of Jerry Cooney, who knocked out heavyweight champ Ken Norton in just 54 seconds into the first round. Only this guy's a little better looking. His broken nose was the only thing that kept him from being handsome. He gave us a broad smile.

"God bless all here," he said, in the standard greeting you'll get in any pub in Ireland, north or south. He took a stool beside us.

"Buy you boys a drink then?"

"Sure," I said, offering my hand. "I'm Fenway Burke."

He didn't take my hand but smiled and nodded. "Guinness for me," he said to the bartender. Then he turned to us.

"I know who you are, Fenway, and you've got to be Tiny Murphy; heard a lot about you as well."

Tiny nodded, but said nothing. The bartender put our drinks in front of us. Cooney raised his. "Here's to ya." Four glugs and he drained it, then set the empty pint glass down on the bar.

"Another?" the bartender said.

"Ah, if only I had the time." There was the look of a wolf about him. His eyes were bright but completely without warmth, like shiny black stones from a cold water stream. Tiny stirred on his stool.

"I'm here on the job." Gone was the lilt in his voice.

I smiled. He didn't smile back. "You know, I thought you were," I said.

"You went through those boys from Lynn like they wasn't even there."

"Yeah?"

He lowered his voice, almost to a whisper. Guy sounded like an Irish Clint Eastwood, but I knew he wasn't taking him off.

"Well, I'm not from Lynn. You're off the case as of right now. Understand? Off." He didn't say another word. He just gave us both the look. He picked up his glass with a paper napkin and wiped it clean, then leaned over the bar and dropped it in the soapy water. He nodded to the bartender, put a hundred on the bar and walked out. He wasn't in any kind of a hurry.

The bartender called after him, but the door slammed shut. I tried to follow him out—nothing doing. He disappeared around the back. I just caught a glimpse of him taking off around the corner on a motorcycle; impossible to get a plate number.

"Must be your lucky day," I said to the bartender as I came back in.

"Yeah." He pocketed the hundred.

"Fuck," Tiny said.

"Won't be getting any fingerprints off his glass," I added. "False beard and ponytail, if I'm not mistaken."

"Looked real enough to me."

"Doubt it," I said.

"You got any idea what the hell the IRA's got to do with all this?"

"Not a clue."

Tiny shook his head, then grabbed his pitcher of beer. Using it like a mug, he threw the whole thing down and ordered another. He wiped the suds off his mustache with the back of his hand.

"Jesus," he said. "Maybe I am Boy George."

CHAPTER 20

"Morning," I said to the receptionist. Decked out in my most respectable tweeds, I flashed her a smile. "I'm Randy Rogers' ride. Can you locate him for me?"

She looked me up and down for a moment. "And you'd be?"

My smile got a lot broader. "I'm his uncle, Fenway Rogers."

I caught a break; the receptionist must have been a Sox fan, she smiled and didn't bother asking for ID. She was a chunky little thing, not long out of school; seemed a little unsure of herself. She looked him up on the computer.

"You'll find him in room two twenty-one. Knock hard. The practice rooms are soundproofed."

I walked down a long corridor, passing a dozen private practice rooms. They weren't what you'd call completely soundproof. These kids were all talented; from the violin to the French horn, every one of them sounded like a prime candidate for Symphony Hall.

Randy Rogers was in the last room on the right. I'm no expert, but it sounded like Beethoven to me.

I knocked on the door but was ignored. He either didn't hear me, or didn't want to be bothered. I walked in anyway. Lost in the music, he played on with his eyes closed. I was sure he had no idea I was standing there.

"So, how was Europe?" I asked.

He came out of his trance and stopped playing. He was a slight kid, spiked dark hair with a little too much mousse. He had on a faded blue button-down polo shirt, frayed at the collar and cuffs—not from use but bought that way; built in "character" or some such. I'd seen the same shirt on a mannequin at Macy's. Randy's chinos had a sharp crease. He wore no socks with his penny loafers. I'll be damned. They actually did have brand new shiny pennies in them. This kid was even more of a preppie twit than I was. Had to admire that.

"Do I know you?"

I smiled and offered my hand. He took it uneasily.

"Fenway Burke,"

"Fenway? Am I supposed to take you seriously?"

"It'd be a good plan. I'm working on the Simpson murder case."

"And just what does that have to do with me?"

"You were a close friend of the victim, were you not?"

"I knew him, but so did a lot of students here, Mr. Burke, or whatever your name is. You're a private investigator, aren't you? Not a policeman."

"How did you come up with that one? I didn't say," I shot back and gave him a sideways look.

He stumbled for a second. "I just assumed," he said. "But I don't have to talk to you."

"I think you do—now or later," I said.

"I'm right in the middle of my practice session." His forehead took on a distinct shine.

I looked at my watch. "How much longer?"

"Am I going to have to call security? The Dean, perhaps?"

"Dean Brown? No need, we're old pals. He's the guy sent me down here."

Rogers pursed his lips. "Just what is it you want of me?"

"Did the police question you about this case?"

"Why would they?"

"You were a constant companion of the victim."

"We were never more than what you'd call casual companions."

"How many times did you see him?"

"Really, Mr. Burke. It was a long time ago."

"Ten times, twenty?"

"I never kept score."

"You were with him at the Other Side the night he was killed, weren't you?" I said. "Do you have a friend now, a special friend?"

"That's none of your business." He stood up. "I'm going to have to ask you to leave."

I laughed out loud. I was being dismissed by this kid.

"Detective Quinn, of the Lynn Police, do you know him?"

"Never heard of him, and—as I said—that will be all."

"I'm the guy who determines that, not you."

The kid tried to stare me down. It was pathetic.

"Do you know who my father is?"

"Nope, but I'm going to be paying him a little visit. That will be all," I said, throwing his words back at him. "I'll be in touch." I smiled and left.

I took another look at the yearbook. Rogers was a member of several cultural clubs and service organizations and was on both the tennis and swimming teams. Nothing unusual there, but one of the clubs got my attention: seemed Randall was a target shooter: pistols. Maybe it meant nothing, but the kid did know how to use a gun.

CHAPTER 21

William Rogers lived out in Dover, just thirty miles west of Boston. Oil, gas, real estate and precious metals; I'd done my research, and the Rogers family hadn't seen hard times since Henry the VIII. They were millionaires when they came over from England two hundred and fifty years ago; old money and then some. I'd set up an appointment through the old man's personal assistant.

I couldn't see the place from the street, and almost missed the winding private road to the estate. About two miles in, I finally came up on it. The manse was a red brick, ivy covered affair that had to have close to forty rooms. There was a broad frontage with two working fountains on either side. I couldn't believe it, but there were two small statues of footmen holding lanterns at the entry. They were in blackface, with broad smiles exposing bright white teeth—a genuine throwback.

The grounds were impeccable. There was a red stable about

a football field's length from the main house, an olympic-size pool, and tennis courts opposite the stable. A crew of landscapers was busy doing its thing.

I pulled into the circular drive and parked.

I only have three suits, but they're all Brooks Brothers. I wore a gray pinstripe in a desperate attempt not to be thrown out before I could tell the elder Rogers why I was there.

I approached a dark mahogany door with gold fittings, at least twice my height,. The door knocker was a lion's head, the size of mine. I opted for the doorbell and was instantly greeted by a butler I assumed must have been lifted from Buckingham Palace.

"Fenway Burke."

He hesitated for a second and then gave me a slight bow. "If you'll follow me, sir, Mr. Rogers is in the library."

The ceilings were twelve feet tall or better, and floor-to-ceiling bookshelves lined two of the walls. The other walls sported big game trophy heads and not just the usual moose, deer and elk, but lions and tigers and bears. Oxblood leather everywhere—over-the-top masculine.

There was an ornate mahogany hutch with glass-windowed doors; the thing had to be nine feet tall. It was filled with golfing trophies—the biggest one occupied its very own shelf. The trophy was over three feet tall and had to be sterling silver; a golfer in mid-swing, standing on a globe. The plaque read, "First Place, Master's Tournament, Dover Country Club, 2006."

Rogers put down his book and stood, offering his hand. I took it.

"Fenway Burke." I handed him my card.

He was eye-to-eye with me, with a full head of pure white hair and a great tan. He wore chinos with a blue shirt, button-down collar and tasseled loafers with no socks. One wrist bore a gold Rolex and on the opposite hand: a diamond-studded pinky ring that somehow seemed out of place. The guy looked like a runner, long and lean, but he'd had some work; the skin around his face and neck was just a little too tight.

"Fenway Burke?" Rogers said.

He took another look at my card. "I assumed Fenway was just a nickname."

"No, sir. It's my Christian name."

He shook his head. "I didn't realize there was a Saint Fenway."

"You're not from Boston, are you," I said.

Before he could answer, a woman appeared from around a corner. I hadn't seen her come in. Half his age, if that; long blonde hair and an absurd décolletage. She was in skin-tight, horse-riding pants and high boots.

"William Rogers," he said. "My wife, Amber."

She took my hand and gave me a little extra squeeze. Her perfume was good but too heavy.

"Won't you sit down?"

I took a wing chair; they sat opposite me on the couch.

"So, just what is it I can do for you, Mr. Burke?"

"As I told your assistant, I'm taking another look at the Simpson case."

"Yes, yes. At first I had no idea what you were talking about, but that's the murder a couple of years ago, the student?"

"That's right."

"Horrible affair, but I'm afraid you have me at a disadvantage.

Just what does this all have to do with us?"

"You didn't know him?"

"No, not that I can recall."

"Your son did, though."

"Could well have; wasn't the victim going to Berkeley?"

"You do remember."

Amber turned to her husband as if looking for direction, but Rogers didn't miss a beat.

"After your phone call, I looked it up on the Internet," he said.

"But you've never met him?"

"As I say, I really have no idea. Randy's a very affable young man. He has a lot of friends."

"He never mentioned him to you? My information is that their relationship was a special one."

I could see the blood rush to the old man's face. "My son attends a music school. He has a God-given talent. That, sir, does not make him a homosexual."

"That's true." I'd never said he was. "But this is the twenty-first century, Mr. Rogers. A sexual preference is not an indictment."

Rogers glared at me. "Any other questions?"

"The arresting officer, Detective Charles Quinn. Do you know him?"

"Of course not, why would I?" Rogers said.

Amber put her hand on Roger's knee.

"Just covering all bases, standard procedure," I said. "The IRA; in the course of your business, have you ever had contact with that organization?"

Amber tightened her grip on his knee.

"You don't mean the Irish Republican Army?" Rogers said.

"That's exactly what I mean."

He laughed at me. "Really, Mr. Burke, this is even more risible than my son being Liberace." He looked at his Rolex. "I'm afraid that's about all the time I have for you. Sorry I couldn't be of more help." He stood up and shook my hand; the interview was over.

I thanked him for his time and headed for the door. Something caught my eye on top of the fireplace, half hidden by a green ivy plant that covered the mantle from one end to the other. It was a walking stick. I picked it up and looked it over.

"What do you think you're doing?" Rogers said.

"Just admiring your cane," I said. "It's a Blackthorne Stick, isn't it?"

Rogers took it from me and put it back. "Just a decoration," he said.

"Yes, I know—an Irish decoration. A shillelagh, right?"

Rogers hesitated for a moment. "It's time for you to leave."

CHAPTER 22

I was back in my office, working the computer and pulling all the information I could on the Rogers Foundation, looking for an IRA connection. I found at least a hundred charities favored by Rogers, more than a few with seven-figure endowments, but nothing screamed IRA. I printed the whole thing out, along with a profile of William Rogers. I'd go over it more thoroughly later.

Then I had an inspiration. There's a web site called Genealogy. com. I'd pull his entire family history. Maybe there'd be something there. I put in his place of birth as well as his son's but immediately ran into a stone wall. Ah, the Internet: all the information you could ever need and a good deal more, but you've got to know how to access it. I can do the basic stuff but I'm no computer jockey. There's a kid who's helped me out along these lines, used to be one of the geeks at Best Buy before he went out on his own. Gene Palan. I'd put him on it.

There were no hits at all on "Mark Sullivan," the third eyewitness and the one I was still trying to track down. No accounts anywhere—no credit cards used—but he did have an extensive rap sheet: all minor busts; no history of violence; no known IRA connection. I'd have Gene do the Genealogy.com thing on him as well. Couldn't hurt. Might help.

I didn't have our bar visitor's name, of course, but I sent along a description of Cooney to a web site for wanted men. They had nothing. There were a dozen photos matching my general description, but none of them was even close to his facial features. Hard to tell with the beard and all, and that might not have been the full extent of it. For all I knew he could have had a false nose and God knows what else.

An email flashed on the screen, just coming in. "Back off" was all it said. I tried to trace the source with no luck. I saved it before logging off; another project for the geek. Just then the phone rang. Caller ID told me it was the Boston Police Department, Station C.

"Good morning, Captain Dolan."

He didn't bother with courtesies. "You ever get together with that witness of yours, Mahoney?"

"Yeah I did as a matter of fact, going to do a follow-up."

"Don't bother. He's dead. Got it right by his mother's front door."

"Jesus, where are you?"

"Her place. Might want to check this one out."

"On my way." I threw on some clothes and rushed out the door.

Lab boys were everywhere. Yellow crime tape stretched from

the parking meters to the tenement. Mahoney lay on his back on the sidewalk. Dolan stood with a clipboard, watching the scene as I approached.

"How'd he get it?" I said.

"Knife through the heart, 'bout as clean a job as you'll ever see—and right in broad daylight." He waved one of the techs over. "Hey, Kenny, tell this guy what you got so far."

He was just a kid, fresh out of school, in a white lab coat. He stood a little straighter when he spoke to me.

"Victim was grabbed from behind. His head was wrenched back, at least two broken vertebrae, and he was stabbed in the heart with one stroke. He was dead before he hit the ground."

"This was not the work of a street punk," Dolan observed.

The tech shook his head. "Classic Special Forces stuff, right out of the textbook. My guess is it was done in one fluid motion."

"Anybody see anything?" I said.

"You kidding?" Dolan asked.

"Where's the mother?"

"Upstairs. They got her sedated, but she don't know nothing," Dolan said.

I shook my head. "The assassination of Peter Mahoney."

Dolan looked up from his clipboard. "Punks like Mahoney don't get assassinated, they get their asses killed. Just what have you gotten yourself into?"

I filled him in on Cooney.

"Political? You gotta be kidding me. What the fuck's the IRA give a shit about these punks?"

"Same question I'm asking myself, Captain Dolan."

CHAPTER 23

I didn't know where I was on the list, but I knew they'd get around to me. The plan was to keep hammering away at the Simpson case and keep Tiny's boys in the picture but out of sight. When Cooney did show up, we'd be as ready as we could be. This guy would be no picnic to sweat, but faced with enough jail time, he just might cough up the names of the people who hired him. Unless it was political; then all bets were off.

I took a ride into Boston and met Megan at the State House, where she'd been meeting with someone at the Office of Victim Assistance.

"What's wrong?" was the first thing she said.

"Remind me never to try to keep secrets from you," I said, and filled her in: the knifing in Dorchester, Cooney, Quinn, Rogers and the rest of it.

"Might be a plan to do what he says," she suggested.

"Drop it?" I asked.

She eyed me for a minute before speaking. "Of course not. It was just a fantasy. You are who you are."

"Got me all figured out, have you?"

That got a little smile out of her. "You're a nut," she said.

"That's how you got me figured."

"It's the only logical conclusion; you're putting your life on the line for someone you describe as one step away from being a cannibal."

"I'm on the job," I said.

"Naturally ... but the trouble is, I'm falling for you. You're the last man in the world I ought to be falling for, but there it is."

"Ditto."

She looked up and smiled. "Ditto? That's it? Ditto?"

I took both her hands in mine, and kissed them.

"You scare the hell out of me," I said.

"But Cooney doesn't?"

"Him I can handle."

"Let's hope so," she said.

"You have any vacation time coming? Might be a good time to take a trip."

"Impossible, I'm already filling in for one lawyer who's taking some time, and another one's on maternity leave. I'm right up to my ears."

"Plan B then."

"Which is?"

"You're being evicted. It's not safe to have you and Spot on the boat. Whiff's going to have to steer clear of me, too."

"And?"

"Already called Tiny. He's got half a dozen men guarding you 'round the clock."

"At work, too?"

"They'll be unobtrusive."

"Ax and his pals; they'll be unobtrusive?"

"Exactly," I said.

CHAPTER 24

I was on my way to Cedar Junction to spend some quality time with my client; maybe he could shed some light on things. It was the usual routine. I was frisked at multiple checkpoints, marched through a metal detector and finally left alone in a windowless room with Mr. Shawn Corbett, who was shackled to a metal desk bolted to the floor. He looked up as I came in, his face expressionless.

I didn't bother with preliminaries, but took the chair opposite him.

"Do you have any connection at all with the IRA?"

There was genuine confusion on his face. "The what?"

"The Irish Republican Army?"

"Are you shitting me?"

"Just answer the question."

"You're fucking crazy!"

"You've got no connection? I have to ask. It's important. Your whole life depends on your answering me honestly."

"I don't know nothing, what the fuck you think?" He tried to get to his feet, straining at his shackles.

I put my hand on his shoulder and gave him a none-too-gentle squeeze. I pushed him back down and then filled him in about Cooney.

"Listen to me, Shawn. Listen good. People are dying because of you and it's a long way from over. You know anything, anything thing at all, you damned well better come clean."

He shook his head. "I'm telling ya, I don't know nothing," he said.

I nodded and kept at him for almost an hour. It was a one-hundred-percent success; he succeeded in convincing me he was telling the truth, and I succeeded in pissing him off.

I smiled and stood. "Thanks for your time, Mr. Corbett." I called for the guard.

"That's it?"

"That's it."

He started to sputter obscenities. I could still hear him halfway down the hall, getting louder and louder. Mr. Corbett was getting out of hand.

r   r   r

THERE WAS A LIGHT DRIZZLE. My office was just around the corner, but I took my little Porsche and parked her right out front. I'd spent more time at the office over the last two weeks than I had in the previous year. I needed to make some phone calls and check my email, see if the computer geek had come up with anything. I turned on the computer and while it was booting up got the Mr. Coffee going. I'd just logged on when I smelled ozone and heard a rapid clicking sound, like an old car trying to kick over with a bum starter. The hair on the back of my neck stood up: bomb.

I hit the door at a dead run and just about tore it off the hinges, taking the full flight of steps in one jump. I hit the first floor landing, wrenched my knee and struggled to keep going. The blast made my ears ring and slammed me up against the wall. The whole building shook and there was a loud crash. My car alarm went off, along with everyone else's.

Dust filled the air. I started to choke and smelled smoke. I was lightheaded but somehow got to my feet and made it out the front door. I felt myself go down to my hands and knees. My Porsche was crushed under debris but her alarm still kept screaming. I looked up. The entire second floor was gone. Bright orange flames jumped close to fifteen feet up. The fire spread fast and roared like a steam locomotive. Thick black smoke billowed into the air. God help anybody who was still in there.

I stumbled down the street. The intense heat singed my back and I went down again. My head started to clear and my hearing was coming back. I was around a hundred feet away now and watched as the building was completely engulfed by flames. My cell rang. I answered it absently. It was Tiny. "I must have missed something," he said at first.

"Hey ... you okay?" he said.

"Yeah, yeah," I said.

I could hear sirens off in the distance.

"What's all that noise?" Tiny asked.

I guess I didn't answer.

"Fen ... What the hell ... "

I came to. "Might want to swing by my office when you get a chance," I said.

"What's—"

"Just swing by," I said.

He didn't respond for a second. "You okay?" he asked again.

"I'm okay."

"Got a call from one of my runners in Lynn. Quinn's bought it, couple in the back of the head."

"Busy boy."

"Huh?"

"Never mind," I said.

"Yeah. ... You sure you're okay?"

"All in a day's work," I said.

"Be there in about twenty minutes," Tiny said, and then hung up.

My knee hurt like hell but I was coming out of it. I leaned up against a black Caddy with a shrieking alarm. I could see flashing blue lights. There were four cop cars headed my way. The sirens wailed as the cars screeched to a halt right in front of what used to be my office. The lead cop waved and headed my way.

"Rough world out there," I said under my breath, stealing an old W.C. Fields line. "Fella's lucky to get out of it alive."

CHAPTER 25

Tiny showed up in less than twenty minutes in a Maserati four-door sedan. He had friends in the car business who liked to gamble.

Firemen tried to keep the flames from spreading to the building next to my office. Tiny whistled and pointed to my car.

"Won't be going anywhere in that for a while."

"Yeah, right," I said.

"They mean business," Tiny said. "Quinn got hit about an hour before they tried to do you. Like to know how the hell they ever got in there to set the damn thing with my boys surrounding the place. I'm gonna have to kick some ass."

"Don't bother." I said. "Guy timed it just right, really threaded the needle," I bit my lip. I still wasn't quite all there.

We headed over to the Quinn crime scene in Lynn. It was on Market Street, right around the corner from The Other Side. The place was a circus, with cars backed up for a mile. A traffic cop was trying to sort out the mess, sending people down Oxford Street, out and around the crime scene. Yellow tape sealed off the area. Tiny parked nearby. I told him to wait for me. Didn't see any sense in introducing him to the cops. I showed my badge and told the cop I had some information. He said I needed to talk to Captain Merritt. I ducked under the yellow tape.

Merritt was in his shirtsleeves with his back to me. He looked down at the body as a tech drew the chalk line around it. Merritt lived over in Swampscott, next town over from me. I'd seen him at Maddie's a thousand times. Quinn was face-down, half his head blown away just above the eyebrows. There was a dark brown circle on the pavement, like a halo. Merritt turned to me.

"I hear you know this guy."

"Charlie Quinn," I said.

"Heard you had a run-in with him."

"Just asked him a few questions."

"You kill him?"

"Nope."

"Got an alibi?"

"I was at Maddie's with Whiff. You know him," I said.

"Yeah, I know him all right. But don't be going anywhere until I check it out," Merritt said.

"Wasn't planning to," I said.

"Anybody else with you?"

"Just the bartender and a dozen other guys."

He took out his pad. "You got their names?"

"Naturally." He took them all down.

"Okay," he said.

"My office just got blown to shit," I said.

"Came over the radio a minute ago," Merritt said, and then looked up from his pad. "Bomb squad'll check it out."

"Won't find squat. It'll burn right to the ground."

Merritt shrugged. "And you figure somehow this is all tied together."

"Sure as hell do," I said.

Merritt stooped down and lifted Quinn's head. "Looks like at least three at close range. Guy got hit from behind, landed face down. Damn brazen, right here on a main street."

"Anybody see anything?"

Merritt shrugged. "This is Lynn. We've got three shell casings, nine millimeter. State cops are on the way. What do you know about all this?"

"Quinn was the arresting officer on a case I'm working on."

Merritt ran his hand through his thick brown hair. "Word is your pal Tiny Murphy's got a hand in this somewhere. Just what's his role ... exactly?"

"Just a public-spirited citizen," I said.

Merritt rolled his eyes.

The sky was gray. The sun tried to break through the heavy overcast. There was a sprinkle of rain, then a sudden wind, whipping up the grit of the inner city. Merritt blinked, something in his eye.

The staties showed up, a Captain Kevin King. I'd heard of him but never met him. Tiny knew him, though. There'd been a beef a couple of years ago that I was a little unclear on, but it had been worked out. The two of them had a grudging respect for each other.

King looked like a Marine officer, with a jarhead cut, thick neck and big hands.

"You're Burke, right?"

"Yep."

"Hear you almost got blown up," he said, without introducing himself.

"Little mishap."

He glanced down at the body. "Let's get some coffee."

We left the crime scene boys to their job.

CHAPTER 26

Andy's is an old-style diner right off Market Street. I halfway expected the coffee to cost a nickel. No such luck; had to admit though, the food smelled damned good. We all ended up ordering breakfast. The three of us took a booth by a widow overlooking the street. Cars finally started to roll by. The traffic cop at the crime scene got them on the move. It started to rain, hard.

The waitress brought our bacon and eggs with home fries. We sipped marginal coffee. The place was the original greasy spoon.

"You think this whole mess is tied to the Simpson case?" Merritt asked.

I told them what I knew and some of what I halfway suspected.

"And you beat the shit out of the guys Quinn sent, but never went after him?" King said.

"Come on," I said.

"Got a guy checking out your story right now," Merritt said.

I shrugged. "Fine."

King turned to Merritt. "Quinn, you got anything on him?"

"We knew he came into some cash, not like he made a big secret of it. Internal affairs never got involved," Merritt said.

King gave Merritt a look.

"Hey, we don't launch a major investigation unless we have a good Goddamn reason. People do come into money on the up and up, ya know."

"Right," King said. "So, Burke, you do a little nosing around and then you get a couple a visits from Washington's boys."

"Right," I said.

"You think they made the move on you because of Quinn?" King asked.

"Yep," I said.

"Why?" Merritt asked.

"Covering his ass, or trying to. The way I see it, he must have gone after the Rogers kid as a possible suspect in the Simpson case. Then he gets bought off. Quinn goes into the computer and comes up with a fall guy."

"Yeah?" Merritt said. "But where's the IRA fit in?"

I didn't say anything for a minute. "Never said I had it *all* figured out."

"No, you didn't." Merritt said. "Be nice if something popped up on Quinn's computer log."

"Doubt it," King said. "He'd be one stupid son of a bitch to not cover his ass that way. Anyway, it's been a couple of years; any record would probably be automatically erased by now."

"Right," Merritt said.

King looked to me. "You started asking questions and Quinn sends in the goons figuring he can make you go away." King said.

"But you're not going anywhere," added Merritt.

"No." I said.

"Then this Cooney guy shows up," King went on, "and the next thing you know Quinn's guys are trying to kick your ass and send you packing."

"That's the sequence," I said.

"Cooney's the hit, then," King said. "But this IRA thing, where's the tie in?"

"Might not be one. Could be Cooney's just a poor Irishman trying to make a living," Merritt said.

"Or not," I put in.

"We'll see if anything comes up on this Cooney of yours," King offered. "You got a name?"

"Sure don't. And I've worn my eyes out looking at mug shots of perps with similar MOs. Got a friend of mine asking around. Could just be he's got some pals who might have used this Cooney before. Something might turn up."

"Tiny Murphy," King said. "Wonderful."

I didn't respond, but just smiled and showed him the palms of my hands.

"Yeah," Merritt said. "And now we've got Mahoney stabbed in the heart, a dead cop and an attempt on your life, one, two, three."

"You're forgetting the other witness, shot in the head by an off-duty policeman," I reminded him.

"Might be just a coincidence," said Merritt.

"I don't believe in coincidences," I said.

"Neither do I," King added.

"Be a plan to do a background on that off-duty cop, see if he has any IRA connection," I suggested.

"Yeah," said King.

"I've been trying to track down the last witness myself," I told them. "No luck so far. He might have already bought it."

"We'll do what we can there, too," Merritt said. "Get the FBI involved. He could be anywhere."

"Got a computer search going, nothing yet," I said.

Merritt nodded. "You figure the Rogers kid killed Simpson?"

"That's my guess. But the only thing I know for sure is my client didn't."

King nodded. "We'll put some men on you, Burke. Long as you keep poking around, you're at risk."

"Won't hurt a bit; got Tiny's boys as my backup, too."

King shook his head. "Quinn was a dirty cop, but he was still a cop. This bullshit won't stand."

I didn't say another word, just smiled and nodded. They were in.

CHAPTER 27

Megan put down the *Salem News* and looked up at me across her kitchen table. Tiny's men were everywhere.

"It says here it was a miracle you weren't killed," she said.

I took the French press coffee pot and refilled both our coffees. "They're just trying to sell papers, wasn't anywhere near as bad as they say."

"I'm not a fool," she told me, slapping the paper. "There's nothing left of the building."

I put my arm around her and sat down. "Hey, I'm in a dangerous line of work. But the police are involved now, not just Tiny and company. It's under control."

She took her napkin and wiped her eyes. "You're sure?"

I smiled and gave her a kiss. "I'm as safe as the situation allows," I said. "For now, just stay inside. Okay?"

She nodded and I gave her a hug.

r r r

FINALLY, A HIT ON MY COMPUTER search: Mark Joseph Sullivan opened a bank account up in Caribou, Maine—about as far north as you can get and still stay in the states. The email gave me both his home address and his place of employment. He was a plumber's apprentice for a local contractor.

"Bingo!" I printed out the information. Caribou was close to twelve hours north of Boston; I had quite a little road trip ahead. No problem. I was actually looking forward to it. Tiny offered me his new Maserati Quattroporte. "Call it a company car," he said. I opted for something a lot less flashy, the big Chrysler Hemi Charger, jet black with tinted windows. It looked like an unmarked police car. That wouldn't hurt me a bit, and she could move. I'd leave a note and sneak out the back door while my cop babysitters were napping.

Before setting out for Maine, I thought I'd make a little side trip, pop in on Mr. Randall Rogers, just to stir the pot. Since the increase in security, all had been quiet on the western front. It was time to shake things up a bit, maybe get Cooney to make another move and expose himself.

The sun was just coming up. I made my escape in the middle of the cops' shift change, shortly before five in the morning. Tiny had the Charger parked around the corner. Throwing an overnight bag in the back seat, I left a note for Megan and hit the road. I stopped at Starbucks in Marblehead and grabbed a dark roast *venti* and a maple frosted scone, the one pastry of theirs I actually like. I took the 128 south to Route 9 west. Randy Rogers had a town house in Wellesley, and I had his class schedule for the day.

The first session wasn't until ten. I'd catch him early. I pulled up in front of the house, looking for the unit number. The town houses were set way back, the grounds well kept. The landscapers had gone a little overboard on the topiary, though.

Rogers answered the door in a silk robe with a cup of coffee in his hand. At first he had no idea who I was. I'm sure I'm the last person he was expecting.

"What? ... What are you doing here?" he said.

I smiled and walked in on him before he had a chance to react. He finally came to.

"What the hell do you think you're doing? You just can't barge in here."

I smiled and took an easy chair in the high-ceilinged room just off the foyer. The floor was a highly polished pink Italian marble.

"We need to talk, Randy. Have a seat." I gestured to the matching chair opposite me. He had no idea what to do, so he looked at me for a minute and then sat down.

"You should have called ahead. I have someone over."

"This won't take long," I said. "Just a couple of things we need to clear up." He took another sip of coffee, no response.

"Couple of days ago someone put three bullets in Charlie Quinn's head, execution style."

"Don't know him."

I smiled. "Of course you do. He was the cop who set up Shawn Corbett for you."

"I have no idea what you're talking about."

"A knifing in Dorchester, very professional. Couple of days later my office gets blown to bits. Your man knows what he's doing."

He took another sip of coffee, trying to stay cool. "Mr. Burke—"

"What's all this costing you, anyway?"

He stood. "That's enough. Get out," he said. He drew himself to his full height: very intimidating.

I leaned back in my chair. "Oh? ... You're not involved in the financial end. I'll have to talk to your old man."

"Am I going to have to call the police?"

"The police? A cop's been killed. I'm working with them, you knucklehead."

He blanched.

We both turned as a slender, young blonde-haired man in pajama bottoms came in. He looked to me, then to Rogers.

"Is everything all right, Randy?" he said.

I stood. "No coffee for me, thanks. I'll just show myself out."

I closed the door gently behind me and felt their eyes on my back as I headed to the car. Randy Rogers was more than a little worse for wear. Mission accomplished.

CHAPTER 28

A couple of hours north, I stopped in Portland for a refill on my *venti*. Portland's the biggest city in Maine. Right on the water, it's bursting with upscale shops and restaurants. It's Maine's answer to San Francisco's Fisherman's Wharf and Boston's Quincy Market. The car's GPS took me directly to Starbucks. I went wild and picked up another maple scone. I'd be leaving my world behind with the Portland city limits and entering the world of flannel shirts, Timberland boots and blue jeans. Figured I'd best be fortified.

I ran up Route 1, no need for the GPS; Caribou is a straight shot, the last stop. Five hours on the road and I got to open her up. Not a car in sight and the blacktop stretched out for miles ahead. I was zipping along at one hundred fifteen and felt like I was crawling. Tiny told me the standard engine in the big Hemi had three hundred and forty horsepower, but he'd told the dealer he wanted a little something extra. I'm no mechanical wizard and I don't know what they did, but this little beauty had something like five hundred and fifty horses and made for one scary machine.

I turned on the commercial-free Sirius radio. I picked up the Sinatra channel and left it there. Getting old, I guess. With ten speakers, it felt like I was in Symphony Hall.

A couple of hours into it, the radar detector went nuts. I slowed to eighty and, sure enough, a couple of miles up a state police car was parked on the left-hand side. Big surprise. You don't often run into state cops this far up. There are maybe eight residents up there, and six of them are moose.

I rolled down my window and flashed the badge the Boston Police issued me when I retired. It has its own leather holding case and is around seven-eighths the size of a standard badge. I kept my fingers crossed and caught a break; the cop just waved me on.

I was about fifty miles south of my final destination when my traceless cell chirped. The MA State Police popped up on the caller ID.

"Good morning, Captain King," I said.

"And where the fuck are you?" he said.

"Running down a lead, of course."

"You're not working alone anymore ... remember?"

"Ah ... but this one requires a bit of finesse."

"Anybody ever tell you you're a wise guy?"

"All the time."

"Burke ... "

"Do I need to point out that I'm trying to get this witness to admit he lied under oath?"

"I know what the hell you're trying to do."

"Well then."

"Well then, what?"

"Guy'll shut up like a clam if you guys show up here with your cement hands, that's 'well what.'"

King didn't respond.

"I'll call you the minute I get things sorted out."

More silence.

"Captain?"

"See the fuck you do."

"Have a nice day," I said.

The phone went dead.

r   r   r

I ENTERED THE CARIBOU CITY LIMITS. The GPS computer voice told me there were no turn-by-turn directions available for my selection, but a map appeared on the screen and the voice directed me to simply follow the arrow as I went along. I drove through downtown Caribou, with its ragged commercial buildings. Half of them were boarded up. I drove six miles north before the arrow had me take a right down an unmarked, rutted dirt road. It looked to be more of a footpath than anything else.

Two and a half miles in, I came to the end. There was a tarpaper shack not much bigger than a good-sized chicken coop, with a rusted stovepipe coming out of the south wall. It was the only house on the road, and there were fresh tire tracks on what passed for the drive. I pulled over to the side as far as I could, trying to get Tiny's car out of sight. Then I turned it around so I could see anyone coming.

And I waited.

I heard him before I saw him, coming around the corner in a battered Chevy pickup. The kid spotted me, too. The driver-side door opened, and he jumped out before he came to a stop, scrambling into the woods. The pickup coughed, then crashed into a pine and stalled. I was prepared for this: had on my brand new Nikes. I took off at three-quarter speed, just to keep him in sight. The woods were thick, but I had no problem staying with him. When I caught up he was sitting on a rock, taking deep breaths. He held up his hands, tried to speak, gave up and shook his head.

I let him get back his wind.

He looked down at the ground. "Get it over with," he said.

"I'm not here to hurt you, Mark."

He looked up quickly. "You ain't?"

I smiled. "I ain't." We went back to his shack.

CHAPTER 29

Mark's place had only one room—no rug on the floor—a pot-belly stove stood right in the middle, and a couple of mismatched beds were pushed against the opposite walls. The only other furnishings were an ancient wooden table and a couple of chairs. There was a kerosene lamp on the table, and an icebox off in the corner. No electricity, naturally, but the place did have a hand pump and a sink half-filled with dirty dishes.

"Nice spot," I said.

The kid shrugged.

"You got a cellar here?"

"Yeah, dirt floor," he said.

I nodded. "That'll do, let's talk down there."

"It's okay, nobody will ever find me up here," he said.

"I did, didn't I? Come on, we'll be out of the line of fire."

He hesitated for a second, grabbed the kerosene lamp and led me down the rickety steps. He lit the lantern, took a seat on a battered steamer trunk and motioned to a wooden crate for me.

Sullivan was a medium-sized kid with olive skin and straight black hair, what my mother used to call Black Irish. He had the start of a full beard, but it was patchy.

I gave him a level stare. "So, who wants you dead?"

He looked me right in the eye but didn't respond.

"I know everything. Quinn, the set up, all of it," I said.

"Why ya want to talk to me then?" His voice cracked, close to tears.

"Couple of loose ends," I said.

"I read the papers, anybody even thinks of talking ends up dead. I'm done with the whole thing."

"Maybe you are, but they're not," I said.

Sullivan fidgeted on the trunk.

"You'll have to come back to Boston with me, talk to the District Attorney."

"Yeah, right."

"There's no running away from it, kid."

"This is my home now. I'm starting over, met this girl," Sullivan said.

"I'm telling you—"

"You ain't no cop. You can't make me go." He started to get up. I put my hand on his shoulder. He sat back down.

"A cop's been killed. I make a phone call, you think they won't come up here and get you? They'd be here right now if I'd let them in on it."

Sullivan just sat there looking at me. His eyes were shiny.

"I wanted to talk to you alone first. Cut you a break if I can."

"Fuck," he said.

"Come clean, kid. It's the only way,"

Nothing.

"Who turned you onto Quinn?"

Sullivan just shook his head.

"I'm gonna have to make that call?"

Sullivan buried his face in his hands. "Brian Cullen," he said. He sounded as if I'd punched him in the stomach.

"Cullen, he's IRA?"

"Yeah, big time."

"What about you?"

"Went to a few meetings. That's how they knew me."

"What's the IRA got to do with all this?"

"I don't know nothing. Ten grand cash for each of the three of us. Cullen said Quinn would tell us what to say."

"You know the other two guys?"

"Yeah, long time. We did exactly what they told us, and then Jimmy O'Shea ends up dead. That's when I took off."

"He got shot trying to rob a 7-Eleven."

"Bullshit," Sullivan said.

I nodded.

"Then it's Mahoney, then Quinn." He started to sob.

"You got any idea where this Cullen is?"

"No, and I don't want to."

I handed him my hanky. He wiped his nose.

"I got a shot up here, learning a trade, staying out of trouble, for once in my life something decent."

I just nodded.

"Asked my boss's daughter to marry me."

"She say, 'Yes'?"

"Yeah." Tears rolled down his cheeks.

"It's okay, Mark. You fucked up, but it's okay." I patted him on the back. He broke down again.

CHAPTER 30

My cell was useless up there. I used a pay phone to tell Megan
I was fine and fill her in. After that I called Tiny about the
break in the case. Shawn Corbett was off the hook; it was just a
matter of getting a deposition on paper. Finally, I called the State
Police.

King came on the line right away. "Where the fuck are you?"

"Just needed a little fresh air," I said, then told him my story.
"Kid says he'll come to Boston for the deposition."

"Yeah?"

"Yes. Tiny's got a half-dozen guys on the way up here to make
sure there's no problem."

"We'll do the same."

"Fine. Tiny's boys will hand them the baton once they show.
Need protective custody for the kid, at least till the Assistant District
Attorney takes his deposition."

"No problem."

"Listen, this kid's got to have immunity."

There was a long silence.

"Not my department. Have him take it up with the DA."

"I told the kid to keep his mouth shut unless he gets something in writing."

"You his lawyer now or something?" King said.

"Just figure he deserves a break. Make sure the ADA has something in writing. Otherwise, no deposition."

"You're a fuckin' piece of work, you are," King said.

"So I'm told. You got anything for me on Quinn's computer records?"

"Hang on a minute." I heard him yell at another cop for a cigarette. "Squat, the system cleared itself months ago."

"What did you come up with on the off-duty cop shot O'Shea?"

"Got nothing, and I mean nothing, but I'll turn in my badge if that deal's on the up and up."

"The cop connected to the IRA?"

"Not as far as we can tell. But get this: the safe was wide open, better than three grand in there and nothing touched."

"That a fact," I said.

"It gets better; three security cameras in the store, and all the VCR tapes have gone missing. Tell me that's not fucked up. The one witness, the clerk? Shot in the back of the head."

"They left you with zero."

"You got that one right. You on your way back down here?"

"Not 'til Tiny's people and yours put in an appearance."

"Good plan."

I stowed Mark in the cellar and stood guard by the window, pistol in hand, waiting for the cavalry to arrive. Tiny and his boys showed up almost eleven hours later, the staties right on their heels. The convoy took off for the Essex County lockup down in Middleton, a dozen cars in all. My new pal Mark had more security than General Patton.

CHAPTER 31

I stopped by Gene Palen's place on the way home. He's my computer geek. Gene was moving up in the world. After leaving his job at Best Buy three years before, he'd started working out of his little apartment. Now he rented space in Marblehead, in what used to be an old boat storage facility. I'd used him a number of times. The guy was tops. There were a dozen dark gray cubicles on the concrete floor—no receptionist, no windows. Two hours working in that place and I'd be a prime candidate for the gas pipe. I stopped at the first cubicle, interrupting a young kid in jeans.

"Supposed to meet with Gene, he around?"

He never took his eyes off the computer monitor, just pointed with his thumb over his shoulder.

"In the basement, number nine," he said.

I walked through the maze. I could have been naked, painted purple with bright orange feathers and no one would have noticed.

I stopped at number nine.

"Hey, Gene," I said.

He looked up from the monitor and smiled.

"Hey there, yourself," he said, standing. We shook hands. Gene had changed his look; still had the jeans but the T-shirt was gone, replaced by a blue Oxford shirt with a tie, no less. He'd kept the chin whiskers, but his hair was shorter, and he'd easily gained thirty pounds. This guy looked like a Republican compared to the kid I'd first met.

"You come up with anything?" I asked.

He must have handed me fifty pages. "Worked on it all day yesterday and most of this morning."

"Anything pop out at you?"

He leaned way back in his swivel chair. I thought he was going to go over backward. He offered me a seat, and then rolled it my way so I could take it.

"Nothing in the family business is the least bit out of order. Taxes are all current. Their holdings are mammoth. The Rogers Family Trust owns or controls over one hundred fifty enterprises, everything from real estate development to toilet seat manufacturing. They've got controlling interest in seven newspapers." He flipped through his copies. "Their first registered business in the United States was a shipping company. That was in 1768. There were over sixty-five merchantmen listed; they traded all over the world, out of Salem. They were filthy *then*."

"Any ties to the IRA?"

"Zip."

"Great." I stood up.

He smiled. I didn't think it was possible, but he folded his hands behind his neck and leaned still farther back in his chair, then looked up at the ceiling.

"Went through their list of charitable foundations, all the usual do-gooder stuff, but ... "

"But?"

"But one of them just may be what you're looking for."

I sat back down.

"The Gallic Preservation Society," he said.

"I checked that out myself; harmless enough, their charter is to foster the use of the ancient Gallic language. They've been major contributors since nineteen thirty-nine."

Sutton smiled. "That's right, but you missed something."

"Don't see how."

"That's why you pay me. It's on another site. They've been investigated quite a few times over the last fifty years for funneling money to the IRA, money laundering. They've always come up clean, but two of the directors actually went on trial in the fifties."

"On the money laundering thing?"

"Nah, nothing tied directly to the Society."

"What was the rap?"

"Gun running, one of them was convicted and got twenty years."

"How'd you make out on that Genealogy.com web site? I got zilch."

"Tough one," Gene said, "birth records in Ireland aren't what you'd call up to speed. But it's clear that William Rogers' grandmother was right from Ireland."

"You got that through US Immigration."

"Bingo."

"Where in Ireland?"

"Ulster."

"Peaceful little community—anything on her?"

"Not really, no record or anything, but she was a Catholic, and she insisted on being married in the church and raising her children that way. The rest of the family was all Church of England."

"You got all that off the website?"

"Took some digging, but yeah," Gene said.

I slapped him on the back. "She must have been a big hit with the rest of the family," I said.

"You bet."

"What about that email? Could you trace it?"

Gene furrowed his brow. "Which?"

"The one warning me off; you were going to trace it. Any luck there?"

He had no idea what I was talking about, and then he remembered. "Right, right, 'Back off.' Yes and no; source was a computer over at the State House."

"The State House?"

"Spammer's trick; it was infected by a virus, then hijacked. Happens all the time, but the guy knew what he was doing: no real trail."

"Great," I said.

"You got anything else for me?" he asked.

"Not at the moment. Just send me your bill."

He sat back down and pulled an envelope out of his top draw.

"Got it right here," he said, and handed it to me.

"Regular genius, you are."

I felt the cubicles closing me in. I needed to get out of that place and clear my head. An afternoon sail, maybe; I got hold of Megan on my cell.

CHAPTER 32

We were three miles out of Marblehead on the *Queen Anne's Revenge*. Tiny's boys shadowed us in a rented forty-foot cigarette boat, ready to jump in at the first sign of trouble. I brushed a strand of Megan's hair off her face. I had my arm around her. She put her head on my shoulder. The sun was bright and warmed my face, but there was a slight sea breeze, just enough to keep things pleasant. It was clear overhead and out to sea, but inland there were gray clouds, getting progressively darker. We could hear occasional thunder, but the weatherman said the storms would never hit the coast. We passed a couple of lobstermen hauling in traps and waved. We were quiet. I was all right with that. I'd filled her in completely on the wrap-up of the Corbett affair. She took her head off my shoulder and looked up at me.

"You think it's over ... really over?" she said.

I gave her a kiss. "My end is anyway."

"And the IRA, they're simply going to go away."

I kissed her on the forehead. "The IRA never had anything to do with this whole mess to begin with."

"Are you a psychic?"

"I'm a realist."

"And what brings you to that brilliant conclusion?"

"Occam's Razor," I said.

"The simplest answer—"

"Usually turns out to be the right one," I finished for her. "Could have been political; maybe they killed Simpson because he was going to spill the beans about their plot to kidnap the Queen. But I doubt it."

"But there *is* an IRA connection. You can't just ignore it."

"I'm not."

Her eyes told me I'd lost her.

"The Rogers kid killed his lover," I said. "I don't know why. Maybe he was jilted. There was alcohol involved, maybe he didn't know what he was doing; I don't know. I do know it wasn't professional. Way too many loose ends; the kid could easily be tied right to the scene."

"So where does the IRA fit in?"

"The local cop was bought off. When that all started to come unraveled, the father turned to the only place he knew, his old family connection. It's not like he's Don Corleone; he doesn't have hit men on staff."

"The father, not the son?"

"Could have been the son, but more likely the old man. Guys like Cooney don't come cheap. It's not like the kid could put it on his platinum card."

"And the old man has cold hard cash."

"Right."

"So this Cooney, or whatever his name is ... he's an independent contractor."

"And a damned good one, but at the moment, out of work. They're having their money problems in Ireland, just like us, but the war's over. The IRA's obsolete."

"Shawn Corbett?"

"A patsy."

"And the Rogers ... they'll get away scot-free?"

"There'll be nothing traceable to the Rogers family, count on that."

Megan took my hand. "You think this Cooney's just going to drop off the face of the earth?"

I gave her another kiss. "That's exactly what I think, once it's officially wrapped up. The guy's a professional. Corbett's off the hook, the Rogers family is in the clear and I'm off the case."

"You're going to drop the whole thing."

"I am."

"Then the Rogers get away with murder."

"Happens every day."

She gave me a look.

"I'll lay it all out for Merritt, but I've done what I was hired to do."

"Yes, you have. And soon Corbett will be back on the streets."

"Yeah, there's that. Makes a fella feel warm all over."

"I'm sure," she said.

"You're sure of all this?" she said.

I took her in my arms and kissed her.

"Looked at it from every angle," I said, holding her close. "'Bout as sure as I can be, without being psychic. You think I'm missing something?"

She shook her head. "You're the detective."

"Right." I gave her another kiss.

Neither one of us said much for a while. We simply leaned back and took in the sights. There was just the slightest chop. The *Queen Anne's Revenge* didn't require any attention; the wind was light, the sails were set and there was no one within a mile of us other than the cigarette boat. After a while, Megan turned to me.

"You're keeping me up nights, Mr. Burke. It's bad for my constitution."

I looked for a hint of a smile. There wasn't any.

"I told you I'm in a dangerous line of work," I said.

"You are, and I'm finding out you're good at it."

"But you'd like me to do what?" I said.

"Something else."

"A career change," I said.

"Astute of you to pick up on my point, I was trying to be coy."

"Not very good at it."

"No," she said.

"Whiff's talked about me working with him. You think that makes sense?"

"Only if you want us to go somewhere," she said.

"I think I do."

Now I did get a smile. "Well then—"

My cell phone chirped, startling me. I thought I'd turned the damned thing off. I could see it was Merritt on the caller ID.

"Sorry, I've got to take this," I said. "Yes?" I could see her watching me, out of the corner of my eye. "Son of a ... but he came in voluntarily and you had him on round-the-clock security. ... Yeah, right. ... I'm on my way." I hung up.

"What is it?" she said.

"Going to have to cut this short," I said.

There was a sudden gust of wind and a quick shower that lasted only a minute, catching us both by surprise. The *Queen Anne's Revenge* rocked as a breaker caught us head on. The dark clouds were suddenly overhead; so much for the weatherman.

"It's Mark Sullivan; he hanged himself in his cell."

CHAPTER 34

When I came in, Merritt was in his office talking with a young woman with long dark hair pulled back and not a trace of makeup, a real crunchy granola type. Next to her stood an older man in coveralls, with a salt-and-pepper beard that stretched almost to his belt buckle. The guy reminded me of Whiff. Merritt turned to me as I came over. I have no idea who the woman thought I was, but she spoke before Merritt had a chance to say a word.

"Mark would never do this," she said. Her eyes were red-rimmed. "We talked the whole thing through."

"You're his girlfriend?" I asked.

"Fiancée," said the beard. "I'm Rod Everson. This here's my daughter, Wendy."

I nodded. "Fenway Burke." I turned to Merritt. "What the hell happened?"

"Found him early this morning, knotted sheet around his neck."

"We need to see the body," said her dad. "Make sure."

Merritt nodded. "Of course," he said. "Come with me. The body's in the morgue."

It was cold and smelled of disinfectant. The attendant pulled out the drawer and unzipped the body bag.

"It's him all right," the beard said.

Wendy stood there paralyzed.

I took Merritt aside. We just stood there for a minute. Neither one of us had any words.

"Any sign of a struggle?" I asked.

"Nothing."

"Cameras catch anything?"

Merritt shook his head. "Power outage in that whole wing for over five hours."

"What the hell?"

"No accident," Merritt said. "That was the only wing affected, three wires neatly clipped."

"Damned professional."

"Sure as hell was. The cut was outside the building, clean as a whistle. Took us a while to find it."

"So that's it, then. The lights go out and the kid ends up dead?"

"No, that's ... What the hell are you saying, Burke?" Merritt's lips grew thin.

"I'm saying I already had a beef with *one* crooked cop."

Merritt moved in fast on me, but stopped himself. He stood there, his face inches from mine, clenching and unclenching his fist.

"You're an asshole. You know that Burke?" he spat the works out between clenched teeth.

"I handed you that kid on a silver platter," I said.

"And I blew it?" Merritt said.

I stared him down. "Like I said."

"Had two guards on him round the clock. What the fuck else am I supposed to do?"

"So?"

"So we find both of them knocked out in front of his cell."

"Drugged?"

"Looks that way. They're in the infirmary. Should have the report any minute."

I nodded and put my hand on his shoulder. I thought he'd brush it off but he didn't. I took a careful look at the body.

"Neck's broken, don't see how that could have happened unless he got a running start. He didn't, did he?"

Merritt shook his head and looked me right in the eye. "No apparent signs of a struggle. We'll have to wait on the autopsy."

"And nobody saw anything," I said.

"Questioning everybody who was anywhere near the scene, but not a goddamn thing. I'll get to the bottom of this. You can bet your ass on that."

"The deposition—" I said.

Merritt cut me off. "Kid refused to sign off on anything until a lawyer looked at the immunity thing."

"That was my doing," I said. "My fault he never signed a statement."

Wendy broke down. "Is that all you care about?" She buried her face in her father's chest. He stroked her hair. "A baby," she said between sobs. "I'm going to have a baby." Then she broke into a primal wail; her whole body shook.

I tried to touch her shoulder, but she would have none of it. I've seen some bad things in my time, really bad; thought I was immune, but I'm not. This one got to me.

CHAPTER 35

Tiny and I were on board the *Queen Anne's Revenge*, moored in her slip. The sky was gray and there was a light drizzle. Dark clouds hovered in the distance. It looked like we were in for some weather. Not many people out on the street, very quiet. I don't know if it was the gray skies or just my imagination, but everyone seemed to be acting like they were at a wake.

The Sullivan matter was under further investigation. He'd suffered a mild concussion, but the ruling was he could have hit his head on the metal frame of his bunk the way down. The cause of death was a broken neck. The initial finding was suicide, but no one was buying it. The investigation was far from closed, but whoever carried out the murder knew what they were doing—no loose ends, no place to go, a genuine dead end.

Merritt was on a rampage. Trace elements of a date-rape drug had been found in the bloodstreams of both guards. The drug itself was odorless and tasteless and could be added to either food or drink without detection. A number of other cops had been dosed as well. It was traced to the chow line at the Middleton County Jail. They were still grilling each and every prisoner and guard who'd been anywhere near the place, but so far nothing had broken.

The delivery boy showed up with a couple of coffees and bagels. Tiny handed the kid a twenty and refused any change. Tiny handed me my order. I nodded my thanks, took off the plastic lid and let the steam wash over my face. Tiny took the seat next to me, overlooking the water.

"Sorry I ever had to get you into this thing," he said. He unwrapped his bagel, got cream cheese all over his fingers and licked it off one finger at a time.

"That makes two of us," I said, sipping my coffee.

We watched the boats bob up and down on the light chop. It was another five minutes or so before Tiny broke the silence. "Now that the kid's gone, you got no place to go, do you?"

"Nope."

"But you're not dropping this thing, are you?"

"No."

"You going to open another office?"

"Nah, figured I'd just work out of the boat."

"How's your car?"

"Intensive care," I said.

Tiny snorted, then grew silent. "Sullivan's girlfriend got to you, didn't she," he said.

"Yes ... she did."

"I've got an organization behind me, but I got nowhere near

the resources Roger's got. You know that as well as I do. We might be biting off more than we can chew here."

"Thought's occurred to me," I said.

"You want out, you're out."

"That thought didn't occur to me," I said.

"You still going after Cooney?"

"Him and the people behind him."

"You might be crazy, but not your fault. It's the Irish in ya."

"Blame it on my ma," I said.

"Just so ya know, got the same problem myself. I'm still in too, and I got your back."

I turned to him for the first time, and smiled. "Took that for granted."

CHAPTER 36

I called Rogers a dozen times. He refused every call. But when all else fails, make some noise. Mr. William Rogers was in for a visit. First thing the next morning, I took a ride out to Dover and pulled off the road as far as I could, about a hundred yards from the entrance to Rogers' private drive. I hunkered down with a coffee and *Moby Dick*. I must have started that novel a dozen times, but Melville is a chore for me. Maybe number thirteen would be a charm. I had a feeling I was going to be here for quite a while. I was right.

It started to rain just after ten. I closed my window to a crack to stay dry. That didn't work out so well. It was hot and sticky. I closed the window, started up the car and turned on the air. I did this off and on all day long.

I was one-hundred-seventy-eight pages into *Moby*, a personal best, when Rogers' limo pulled out of the drive. I looked at my watch: four-forty-two. I fired up the Chrysler, let a couple of cars get ahead of me, then fell in behind. Normally on a tail I'd be driving something a lot more nondescript, but in this case, I couldn't care less if he spotted me. In fact, that prospect just might make things more interesting. They took the 128, getting off at Route 9 and pulling into the Chestnut Hill Mall, right in front of Bloomingdale's. Rogers got out, and spoke to his chauffeur. I parked three rows over and followed him into the mall.

He was looking at a pair of gold-flecked pleated slacks. I came up behind him and put my hand firmly on his shoulder. He spun around, completely surprised. Guess he hadn't spotted my tail after all.

"Remember me, Rogers?" I asked.

He eyed me up and down, gathered himself, then stood a little straighter and looked me right in the eye.

"I have nothing to say to you," he said.

"Of course not."

There was a long silence. This was a fellow not used to confrontation.

"All right then. Get it out, what do you want?"

"Your ass," I said, and smiled.

"Just who do you—"

"I'm putting you on notice, Rogers—this thing isn't going away, not as long as I'm around."

He got red in the face. "You're a fool," he said, then turned away from me.

"And you're a murderer." I had nothing else to say. I headed back to the car.

CHAPTER 37

Just after five in the morning, Tiny and I were sitting at the counter of Annie's Diner in Marblehead having coffee. Whiff showed up as we were ordering breakfast, slapped a fifty on the counter and placed his order as well. I gave him the abbreviated version.

"Why not just paint a target on your forehead?" Tiny said.

"Thought I did."

"You sure you know what you're doing?" Whiff asked.

"Open to suggestions."

"Nothing on this guy, Cooney?" Whiff asked.

"No name, no police record, no known associates, no last address; it's like the guy never took up residence on planet earth." I said, then turned to Tiny. "Your contacts come up with anything on him?"

"Went right to the top," Tiny said.

"Rhode Island?"

"Where else?"

"And?"

"The Italians aren't saying nothing."

"Big surprise."

"Hey, something's gotta break. If he is out there and working, he's going to piss somebody off sooner or later."

"I'm hoping for sooner."

"Who ain't?" Tiny asked.

"So, in the meantime, you can't go to him, you make him come to you?" Whiff said.

"Got to go way past full alert, but can you see any other plan?"

Whiff polished off his coffee and motioned for a refill. "Nope. Just so's you're ready for him, that's all."

"Ready as I can be. I need you to double up on the boys, Tiny."

"This is costing me more than I wantta lay out," Tiny said.

I gave him a look. "You backing out on me?" I said.

Tiny didn't say anything for a full minute, then shook his head. "Nah, screw it, I'm still in," he said.

"All right, then," I said. "I've got a security guy setting up more cameras, no way anybody can get near the boat without us knowing it. I've got some underwater motion detectors being installed right now."

"Underwater?" Whiff said. "Little overboard, ain'tcha?"

"Ask Mr. Sullivan."

That shut Whiff up.

"Snipers?" Tiny said.

"Merritt's got men on just about every other rooftop. State cops aren't sitting on their hands either."

"But your ass is still out there."

"Nothing's one hundred percent."

"What's that Megan got to say about all this?" Whiff said.

"Getting her out of the line of fire; a little vacation time, down in the islands. Couple boys keeping an eye on her down there."

"You think Cooney will try to get to you through her?" Tiny said.

"Who knows? But she didn't give me any grief when I put her on the plane."

"Smart girl," Whiff said. "You figure she'll be around after all this blows over?"

My breakfast arrived; three eggs over easy, bacon, toast and crispy home fries. It was the low-cholesterol special. Guess I felt like living dangerously.

"That, me boy, is the sixty-four thousand dollar question. She thinks I'm nuts."

"Like I say," Whiff said. "Smart girl."

r   r   r

OVER A WEEK INTO THE WAITING game, and still nothing, I slept with a pistol under my pillow. This was getting old. I polished off the last of my coffee, got Rowlf and Blanche's leashes and took the kids for a walk. I passed three of Tiny's men before I'd gone twenty-five feet, and then Ax stepped out from behind a parked panel truck, nodded and bent down to pat the dogs.

"Anything happening?" I said.

"Nah, Tiny wants to talk to you though. He's over at Maddie's."

It wasn't even ten-thirty. "Getting kind of an early start, isn't he?"

Ax shrugged.

I was fastening their leashes to an old hitching post when the bartender stuck his head out.

"It's okay, Fenway, they can come in," he said. "We're not officially open 'til eleven-thirty."

Tiny turned on his stool and scratched their ears, then looked up.

"Buy you a beer?" he said.

"Little early for me."

We sat there looking at ourselves in the mirror for a couple of minutes.

"Thought your boy'd turn up by now," he said.

"He'll come all right. I'm being watched."

"No one's spotted him."

"Didn't expect they would. He's not working alone."

"How you figure?" Tiny said.

"'Cause he wasn't in jail with Sullivan, for one thing. Not to mention Quinn and Mahoney buying it so quick back-to-back."

"He had plenty of time to get to both of them," Tiny said.

"But he'd have to know exactly where they were, wouldn't he? He's got people, no question."

"So what's he waiting for?"

"Opportunity. Wants to catch me alone."

"You telling me you want us to bug out of here?"

I laughed and slapped him on the back. "Big man, I'm not suicidal. Going to start taking boat rides. All by my lonesome, every single day at the same time, hand him a regular train schedule."

"Then we come in the nick of time and help you out."

"Something like that."

"He'll see through that,"

"Course he will, but it's the only shot I'm giving him."

"He could hit you from anywhere ... rocket launcher, maybe."

"Rocket launcher?"

"You rule that out?" Tiny said.

"I rule nothing out with that guy. But I don't see him doing this thing long distance. He'll want to get in close. Make sure he does the job on me."

"Hope you know what the fuck you're doing."

"Makes two of us," I said.

"The smart move would be for Rogers to drop it," Tiny said. Anybody connected is dead, and we got no idea where this Cooney is, or who he is for that matter. He disappears, Rogers' one hundred percent in the clear. Why take the risk?"

The bartender brought Tiny a beer and me a water.

"It made no sense to do the job on Sullivan, either. If he'd left the kid alone, that would have been the end of it right there."

"Merritt still would have been on his case."

"You kidding me? Rogers would just throw money at it. His lawyers would be all over him. He might have made a little noise but it's not like he had any place to go with it."

"So how come you figure Rogers won't drop it now?"

"Because he's not as smart as he thinks he is. I've got nothing, but I'm in his face. Hell, I call him six times a day."

"Ever get him on the phone?"

"Nope, but he knows I'm there."

Tiny nodded. "So you figure eventually he'll try to swat his little gnat?"

"I'm counting on it."

"Here's hoping he gets a move on soon. I can't keep this up forever. I got earners off the street and it's costing me money. Got myself a business to run."

I clicked mugs with him. "Time and tide," I said.

"Fucking A," Tiny said.

CHAPTER 38

After taking the *Queen Anne's Revenge* out at dawn every day for a week, I was beginning to think that maybe Rogers had made the smart move and was simply letting it go. I got up early again and made myself a pot of French roast. Brushed my teeth and threw on shorts, sweat shirt and boat shoes. Coffee in hand, I hit the deck and fired up the diesel. The engine's on a delay switch for safety. There's a slight pause, then a warning bell before she kicks in. Ax was deckside before the bell stopped ringing. The diesel turned over and I offered him a coffee.

"Just had one," he said.

He and the boys had two thirty-eight foot cigarette boats and a Scrabe boat the same size, all with twin gasoline engines, moored right next to me.

"You got the fleet all gassed up?" I said.

"Last night. Took care of it myself."

"This could be the day," I said.

"Yeah, you say that every day."

"Yeah ... well. Going out a little farther. 'Bout ten miles. We'll see what happens."

Ax nodded. "We'll be waiting on your call," he said, and headed back to the closest cigar.

I cast off and motored out of the harbor, threading my way among the other craft. Once out in the open, I shut her down and hit the switch to put up the self-furling sails. The wind snapped them taut. The boat rocked on a swell and then responded beautifully. In no time I was crashing through the waves and getting soaked with salt spray even where I was, way back at the wheel. I sailed into the wind and she heeled sharply over to port with water rushing in through the gunnels, then washing right out again. I looked at the gauge. I was hitting almost ten full knots, which was flying for a craft like her. The rigging was singing. Before I knew it I was out close to the ten miles I'd planned on, but saw nothing out of the ordinary.

The sound system came on full blast, playing Wagner's *Ride of the Valkyries*. I jerked my head around, my whole body tensed. I could feel my heart pounding, and then Whiff stuck his head up out of the hatch.

"Figured we could use a little music!" he shouted over the French horns and crashing cymbals.

I took a deep breath. "What the hell are you doing here?" I yelled at him.

"You got to learn to relax, young fella."

"Whiff—"

"Tied one on last night, sacked out in the aft berth."

"And no one saw you?"

"Course they did, but I ain't the enemy. What you think?"

"I think you got no business out here, that's what I think. Too damned dangerous."

Whiff looked around. There was not another boat within a mile.

"U-Boats maybe, but I'm willing ta risk it. You want a rum punch? Hair of the dog."

"I'm heading in." I turned the wheel hard to port.

"Killjoy," Whiff said, and then went down the hatch.

Ax was going to get his ass kicked for whoever let Whiff come aboard without my knowing it. I scanned the horizon: still nothing. Whiff joined me on deck with a rum punch in each hand and offered me a glass. I took a pass and had another look around: still all clear.

"Suit yourself," Whiff said. "Anyway, good day for a sail." He tossed one of the punches back and started on the other, then laughed and mussed my hair. "Might as well enjoy it, no harm done."

I thought about it for a minute and smiled in spite of myself. "Just don't ever pull this bullshit again," I said.

Whiff held up his hands, "On my word of honor," he said.

"Right."

We were still close to five miles out. Whiff talked about everything from baseball scores to the price of cod racks for lobster bait to my childhood growing up in Marblehead.

I caught some movement out of the corner of my eye. It was a lobsterman off in the distance. Behind him was a cigarette boat, heading in the same direction.

Whiff pulled out the binoculars and took a hard look.

"Lobsterman's Hank Ales, he's okay." He still held the glasses to his eyes. "Don't know the guy in the other boat, but I see them out all the time. Stepping right along, but those cigarettes always do."

I grabbed my binoculars from Whiff. The cigarette boat was a big one, had to be a sixty-plus footer, coming on strong. I couldn't make out the man on deck, but he was a big guy and all in black. I got on the radio right away and called Ax and the boys. They'd be on the scene exactly when I wanted them to be. I turned to Whiff.

"Got a couple of AK-47s below, right under my bunk. Grab 'em, will ya?"

"Ya think—"

"Just do it," I said.

Whiff disappeared down the hatch.

The cigarette picked up speed, hit a wave and went airborne, coming down with a huge splash and cresting another roller before taking off again. He was still close to a mile off, but with the glasses, I could see him clearly now: Cooney.

The radio crackled. "Fenway, we're dead in the water!"

"What the fuck are you talking about?" I shouted into the mic.

"Started up fine," Ax said. "Couple hundred yards out, all three stalled. Can't get them started!"

"I need you out here, now!" I yelled, and then threw the mic aside and yelled for Whiff.

"Let's get a move on!"

"Coming!" he yelled back, but took a few more minutes. Cooney was on us in a flash. Whiff's head popped up out of the hatch.

"Only found one!" he shouted, and then he tossed me the AK.

"Get below!" I yelled. I got off a few rounds peppering Cooney's boat. He returned fire, looked like he had an M-59, a combination machine gun-grenade launcher. The bullets tore up the hull all around me, passing right through. Had to be armor piercing. I continued to chew up his boat with the AK.

Cooney let loose with the first grenade. The blast knocked me hard into the steel wall, rattling my teeth and bouncing me down the hatch. I landed hard on my back, the wind knocked out of me. It felt like my right side had caved in; no feeling at all from my shoulder down. Something warm and sticky ran into my eyes. I blinked, trying to focus. There was a metallic copper taste in my mouth and everything was a blur. Black smoke poured out of the hatch. The *Queen Anne's Revenge* shuddered as three more grenades hit in rapid succession.

I tried to shout but it came out more of a croak. Whiff moaned as I tripped over him. The smoke cleared just enough to make out my surroundings. He was pinned under the engine; the hull was cracked all along the side. Water was rushing in and we were already starting to list to starboard. Whiff's mouth and chin were covered in blood.

"Aw, Jesus," was all I could say. I went to my knees and touched his face.

He looked up. "Back's broke," he said.

"My fault ... my fault, never should have let you come." I couldn't help it. I started to cry.

"You didn't." He was strangely calm. "It's okay, kid. ... Had a good run." Then he smiled. "Love you like a son, always have." He was still breathing, but he closed his eyes.

There was a burst of fire and a metallic ringing, and suddenly the sun poked though a couple of dozen bullet holes. I instinctively ducked down as Cooney chewed us up. I had to get him off us.

My head was spinning. I thought I was going to throw up. I grabbed the ladder for support and somehow clambered my way up to the deck. I stumbled, but regained my footing and used the rail to balance the rifle. I was seeing double and my right arm was useless, but he was less than a hundred feet away. I opened up with a long burst which shattered his windshield.

I saw him duck for cover. Then I opened up on his aft. Instantly he started to trail thick black smoke. I'd taken out one of his twin gasoline engines. I stood up higher to get a better angle and went for his gas tank. Two Donzi speedboats were less than a mile away. Had to be Ax and the boys. Cooney would be forced to break off the attack. He let loose a final burst on the fly.

The first shot hit me high in the left shoulder, turning me around, the next just above my liver. The third took out a rib and spun me around in the opposite direction. A sharp shard of stark white bone stuck out of my chest. I felt myself being lifted off the deck and then falling back; then, nothing but blackness.

CHAPTER 39

It smelled like ammonia and disinfectant. I heard disconnected voices, followed by short periods of silence. Blurred shapes moved all around me in black and white, sharp jolting bites of pain, followed by a weariness I had never known in my entire life. I became conscious of a steady pulse, at times drowning out all else. There was a bright white light, hot, so hot. I closed my eyes against it. My eyes stung. I blinked but it didn't help. I tried to speak, but my throat felt like it had been reamed out with a plumber's snake. I closed my eyes tight then opened them again. Someone was standing over me, a hefty woman dressed in white with short blond hair.

"Well, look who's come to say hello," she said, then wiped my brow with a cool damp cloth. I smiled but couldn't lift my head off the pillow. An IV taped to the back of my hand throbbed slightly. I was still among the living. I hurt all over. I tried to speak again but still couldn't.

She leaned down and put her hand on my shoulder. "Give it a rest," she said. "You're not all the way back yet."

It wasn't until late in the afternoon that they took the tube out of my throat. I gagged, and then went out again. Next thing I knew the bed was cranked up and Tiny was opposite me reading *Car & Driver*.

"Where am I?" I said.

"Salem Hospital," Tiny said, and then put down the magazine.

"Whiff?"

He touched my hand.

"Sorry, Fenway, went down with the ship. Regular miracle you're not with him."

I felt my eyes fill up.

"Ax is all busted up over it for letting him spend the night. Thought you knew he was on board and you'd kick him off before you went out."

"Yeah ... " I bit my lip. "It's like Whiff said, just one of those things."

We were both quiet.

"How long have I been here?" My voice sounded like a stage whisper.

"Twenty three days. Got you registered as Edward Teach."

"Black Beard," I said. I managed a little smile.

Tiny smiled back. "Thought you'd appreciate that—fought like him."

"Don't remember much. ... Wait a minute, what the hell happened to your boats?"

"Sugar in the gas lines," Tiny said.

"When they gassed up," I said.

"Yeah, damned slick, fouled right at the source. Ax filled up just as they were closing. Nobody reported any problems till the next morning. Then half the damn marina was out of action."

"Son of a bitch."

"Yeah," Tiny said. "Son of a bitch."

"Started to work its way into the lines on the way back to the slip."

"That's how they figure it, yeah."

"They must have been watching you and phoned it in the minute you went out. The cigarette was rented a couple of weeks before at fifteen hundred a day. First day she ever went out was the day you got hit."

"We grabbed a couple of Dozis and gave chase but he had too much of a head start. They found his boat abandoned in Lynn Harbor. Hope the fella rented it out had good insurance. Shot to hell."

I nodded. "I do remember bits and pieces."

"Don't go looking at the newspapers. The Globe ran your obit; didn't want Cooney blowing up the hospital. Merritt set it all up."

"I'm a dead man," I said.

Tiny smiled and touched my shoulder. "For now, anyway.

I nodded but my eyes were growing heavy. "Megan?"

"She'll be right back."

I could feel myself fading. "She's here?"

"We got her in undercover. Don't worry; if there was a tail, we shook it. Right at your side the whole time. Just went to get us some coffee."

I couldn't keep my eyes open any longer—lights out.

WHEN I CAME TO IT WAS DARK. Megan leaned over and gave me a kiss and a hug. I tired to hug her back, but there was nothing there. I did manage to get my arms around her. It took a lot out of me; any little movement made me lightheaded. She held me for the longest time, then unwrapped my arms from around her, kissed me gently once again and sat down beside me. There were tears in her eyes.

"Thought I lost you," she said. She put her hand on top of mine.

"Missed you."

"Me too."

"Am I going to make it?"

"You'll survive."

"Weak as a kitten, no feeling at all on my right side."

She touched my arm. "Doctors say that's normal."

A young Asian man in a white coat with a stethoscope around his neck came in. His hair was slicked straight back. He was slight and just over five feet tall. Captain Merritt and Tiny came in right behind him. Merritt just gave me a nod.

"I'm Doctor Lin," he said. "How are you feeling today?"

"Like someone shot the shit out of me."

He smiled. "Fair enough. I can come back later if you like."

"That's okay," I said.

He took a seat at the foot of my bed. "I'm the surgeon who operated on you. You're one lucky guy."

"Not feeling like one," I said.

"Trust me. Hit three times, no vital organs damaged. One of them missed your spine by a millimeter."

I smiled. "There's a break."

"Here's another: armor piercing rounds. Conventional rounds would have expanded on impact, blown you right in half. These passed right through you, clean going in, clean coming out."

I just nodded.

"Trauma on your right side from the explosions. I had to remove your spleen. You suffered a severe concussion." He looked at his clipboard. "Let's see here ... five cracked vertebrae, three broken ribs, one of them a compound fracture, broken hip ... you've got a titanium pin holding it together ... assorted cuts and bruises requiring almost four hundred stitches." He put the clipboard down. "That's about it."

"Will I ever run the high hurdles again?"

"Not for a while," he said. "Some of it may never come back. We'll start you with a therapist, just stretching, and then move you along to simple exercises. After that, your second home had better be the gym. You have one long convalescence ahead of you."

"How long?"

"That depends on how hard you work, but I think you're looking at least a year."

I looked to Megan. She gave me a tight smile.

"Great," I said.

Lin patted me gently on the shoulder. "I'll check in with you later." He took his leave.

Merritt took my hand. "Never laid a glove on ya," he said.

"Right," I said.

"I got just one question. ... Who did it?"

"Cooney."

"You get a positive ID."

"It was him all right."

"The boat went down in over eight hundred feet of water. Far as the Globe's concerned, you're down there with her." Merritt put a copy of the paper down on the bed. "Not many guys get to read their own obit," he said.

I nodded, barely able to keep my eyes open.

"Got the place crawling with cops. Nobody, but nobody, can get to you in here. I don't give a fuck who he is."

"Hospital's got to be asking questions," I said.

"Far as they're concerned, it's national security," Merritt said.

"They buy that?" Tiny said.

Merritt shrugged. "Got Steve Boyle to have a little chat with the hospital administrator."

"Boyle?" I said.

"Used to be on the force. He's with Homeland Security now," Merritt said.

"You get all this cleared upstairs?" I said.

"Hell no, it's is all on me. The fewer people in on this the better. Don't have to worry about the hospital. They don't know who the hell you are."

"What are you doing about Cooney," I said.

"I've got an APB out on him, but he could be anywhere. It's not like we can put up roadblocks."

"So ... for practical purposes, as far as your guys are concerned, this case is closed," I said.

"Let's just say it's on the back burner. One bright light: internal affairs is opening an investigation into Quinn's handling of the case. With luck, your boy Corbett will be in the clear."

"This isn't about Corbett anymore."

"Yeah," Merritt said. "Well, for now at least, long as this Cooney thinks you're dead, no one around you has anything to fear."

"Lay low," I said.

"That's the plan."

"For now."

That was it for me. I'd come back to fight another day, but for now, I was down for the count.

CHAPTER 40

I couldn't have walked if I tried, and it was hospital procedure to check me out in a wheelchair. Tiny pushed me down the corridor to the elevator. I don't know, I was glad to finally get the hell out of there, but something about not being able to leave on my own power really got me down. Megan picked up on it right away as she walked by my side. A smile played on the corners of her lips.

"Cheer up, will you?" she said. "You're going on extended vacation."

"Where to?" I said.

"St. John," said Tiny. "US Virgin Islands. No passport needed, private plane, no paper trail. Taking a couple of weeks myself."

"St. John?" I said.

"Got a place down there," he answered. "A cruising cat too. You've had an influence on me."

"You, a catamaran?" I said.

"Fifty-six-footer, got a deal from a place called the *Moorings*. They lease her out when I'm not using her. According to the salesman, I'll actually make money."

"Good luck with that."

We took the elevator down to the basement, where we were met by Ax and his crew. "Thought they'd be shipping you out of here in a body bag," he said.

I turned to Megan. "Guy really knows how to light up a room, doesn't he?"

Tiny lifted me into a black Lincoln Navigator that was half the size of a Greyhound bus. I was up front, with Tiny at the wheel. Megan sat right behind me; Rowlf and Blanche shared the rear with Spot.

Lucky I'm not all that sensitive, because there wasn't much of a reception from the canine kids. Rowlf and Blanche looked, gave their tails a little shake, and then promptly put their heads down again. Must have been nap time. Spot wasn't a whole hell of a lot more enthusiastic than my own mutts. Guess I should have brought along some treats; would have gotten the red carpet treatment then.

Ax and company were in identical SUVs. They drove with us to the airport, one in front, one behind. Megan gave Tiny the evil eye.

"You never heard of Al Gore?" she said.

"Global warming's a myth," Tiny said. "Saw it on the Internet."

"Tiny, please, I'm begging you, don't start." I said.

Tiny laughed. "Let ya off the hook, but only because you're in a debilitated state."

"I owe you," I said.

"You ain't seen nothing yet," Tiny said.

The airport was a breeze: no security check, no lines, nothing. Tiny had another one of his deals going. I thought he was nuts when he'd first told me about it a year or so before, but he had what amounted to a timeshare on a Lear Jet. God forbid Tiny should ever have to fly first class. "Might as well mail myself parcel post," he said.

I had to admit it was an experience. I felt like King Farouk. The cabin resembled an oversized Rolls Royce, with its flawless leather and teak trim, and our stewardess was a dead ringer for Keira Knightley. She served us champagne and Beluga caviar, and talked intently with Megan all the way down. Turns out she was a graduate student at Harvard.

"I could get used to this," I said.

Tiny clicked his glass with mine. "Might as well. You can afford it."

"I think you're confusing me with someone else," I said.

Megan interrupted. "I didn't tell him, Tiny."

Tiny nodded. "Your inheritance. Turns out Whiff was a savvy investor; you got the business, twenty-six working boats in all, free and clear. It's a trust, so it's as clean as a whistle, no probate."

"And just over two million in stocks and bonds," Megan said.

I lost my breath for a moment. "I'm a dead man, remember?"

"It's all on hold for now," Megan said. "I've got an associate who can sort out the legal end once you get back."

It took a minute for everything to sink in. "So, I'm rich. Not in your league, Tiny, but—"

"Very handsome man with his wallet on," Tiny said.

"It's not that way at all," Megan said.

"Don't hurt though," Tiny said.

Megan laughed. "I won't hold it against him."

CHAPTER 41

Tiny's condo was in a section of St. John called Red Hook. High on a mountain, it overlooked the ocean, St. Thomas, St. Croix, and a dozen other smaller islands even Tiny couldn't identify. The building was tan stucco with a touch of gold and had a bright red tile roof; it looked down on a private, pristine sugar sand beach, dotted with palms. I have no idea how many square feet, but the condo was good-sized: three bedrooms, two and a half baths. Tropical vegetation surrounded it. The landscaper must have had a thing for bougainvillea; red flowers everywhere and purple ones that looked like bottle cleaners. No one around; it was off-season. The ocean views were spectacular.

"Who said crime doesn't pay?" I said.

"Nah, I'm legit now ... mostly," Tiny replied. "Getting driven out by a bigger outfit." He started to wheel me to the front door, Megan by his side and the kids bringing up the rear.

"I didn't think there was a bigger outfit," I said.

Tiny snorted. "State of Massachusetts, and they call *me* a crook."

"Law enforcement?" Megan said.

"State lottery commission," Tiny said. "First they take over the numbers racket and leave me with nothing but off-track betting, and by this time next year, that'll be gone too."

"Middleborough?" I said.

"Yep, first Middleborough, then Palmer. Two casinos in two years; three more proposed, all perfectly legal and licensed by the state. Getting harder and harder for an honest businessman to make a dollar around there."

Tiny opened the front door. Megan looked inside. The highly polished white marble foyer led out to an expansive living room with a cathedral ceiling that had to be close to twenty feet high. Potted palms were big enough to climb. The wall facing the ocean was glass.

"Poor baby," she said.

Tiny laughed. "Well, you know, we all have to do what we can."

ᚱ   ᚱ   ᚱ

I WAS WALKING LIKE AN OLD MAN, stooped and achy all over, but I was moving unassisted and that was something. I started working out with two, four-pound dumb-bells, doing curls, reverse curls, tricep and chest extensions on the bench. It hurt like hell and half the time Tiny had to help me out toward the end of my set.

Scary. Before my little boat trip, I'd regularly worked out with fifty pound dumb-bells and bench pressed up to eight plates, four hundred-five pounds. I was a long way from even moving the bar with no plates at all, and that's what Megan used, just for her warm up. I was shocked at my weight. I'd gone from two ten to one seventy-five. I hadn't been under one-eighty since high school.

We had a regular little routine down, stretching first thing in the morning after coffee and a light breakfast, then to the heavy bag and the weights. I'd take long breaks between sets, head down, hands on my knees. My endurance was completely shot. I couldn't last sixty seconds on the bag, and it was almost all hand work. I'd manage a couple of light straight kicks, but I couldn't reach above waist high, and it was strictly pitty-pat, nothing at all behind it. Roundhouse kicks were completely out of the question. Couple of hours of that and my arms would be trembling; nothing left, nap time.

An hour after lunch we were on the beach; lots of protein, branched chain amino acids, creatine and a half-dozen other bodybuilding supplements, all approved by the doc. I'd do a walk-run thing with Tiny, Megan and the dogs literally running circles around me. The sand was hard-packed and perfectly flat. Had I been sinking in, I doubt I could have made it one hundred yards. Even as it was, I was forced to take frequent breaks. My right side hurt like hell whenever I tried to push any weight, but it was a good pain now. I knew I was on the mend.

We'd wrap up around three. I'd take the golf cart up the steep slope to Tiny's place, trailing the rest of the crew as they wrapped the workout by sprinting to the top. Tiny stayed a third week. I'd abandoned the cart and took my first attempt up that hill at a labored walk. I had to stop six times, gasping for breath and dripping with sweat. I rested at benches strategically placed on the side of the winding drive, but I made it. They were waiting for me at the summit and greeted my like some kind of Olympic hero. I felt like one, too.

We'd head down to *Mongoose Junction* for dinner, with its fashionable boutiques, restaurants and watering holes right on the water. Tiny introduced us to *Cruzan Rum*, a local favorite. My limit was just one, and that was touch-and-go, but I had no problem with the spiny lobster and all the rest that went with it. Whiff had always put a bad rap on the warm-water variety and I could see his point, but I came to the conclusion that that was unfair. It wasn't apples to apples; the New England lobsters and the Caribbean variety were just different animals all together, as simple as that. I was putting on muscle and getting myself a killer tan.

Megan reached over and touched my hand. "You're making amazing progress," she said.

"Damned right," I gave her a peck. "Hitting the pistol range tomorrow.

She blanched.

"You okay?

"She fumbled with her napkin and then took a sip of rum punch. "Sometimes I wish you were making a little less progress."

"Megan—"

"You're not indestructible. Haven't you figured that out yet? He'll kill you the next time. I know it."

"I can take care of myself," I said.

"Just forget it." She teared up. "I'm going to take a walk." She left us there.

Tiny and I watched her walk away, neither one of us saying

a word. He polished off his drink and waved to the waitress for another. "How 'bout you?" he said, pointing to my half-filled rum punch.

I broke my rule. "What the hell," I said, and drained the last of it in one swallow.

"Can't blame her," Tiny said. "He's a scary guy."

"She's afraid of losing me," I said.

Tiny leaned his chair back, putting it up on two legs. "Oh yeah, I can see how that would scare the hell out of her, chick like that."

"Tiny—"

"She ain't got much to offer. It could take her two ... three *weeks* to get a replacement."

The waitress came with our drinks. Tiny polished off his old one and started in on the new one.

"Thanks a lot," I said.

We clinked glasses. "Don't mention it."

"It's not like I can just let him go. What's she want, anyway?"

"She wants you to be someone else," Tiny said.

CHAPTER 42

I was out, rain or shine, seven days a week, both at the pistol range and hitting my workout routine hard. It was slow, but I was making progress. I went from a walk-stop-walk, to a jog-stop-walk-jog. Rowlf and Blanche ran fifty yards or so ahead of us, then hunkered down and waited for me to catch up. Thank God for the hard-packed sand.

I was up to six full minutes continuously on the heavy bag with hand work, straight kicks and even managed to get a few of the roundhouse variety in. Before the incident on the boat, I could easily go a full half-hour, beating the living hell out of that thing. I still didn't have a whole lot behind my punches, but every once in a while I'd rock that bag pretty good. Sometimes I even managed to do the full heavy bag work out without puking my guts. ... Sometimes.

Megan spent the first two weeks with me and then went back to Boston with cases to attend to. She promised to be back on St.

John the following week, but it didn't happen. She told me she needed time. I figured I'd give her a break and confined my contact to daily emails. I didn't like it, but there wasn't much else I could do in the shape I was in. Tiny had some business up in Boston and left me with Ax, who pretty much left me to myself. I didn't mind. No one was going to get near me without them knowing about it. I spoke to the big guy almost every day by phone, and, before I knew it, three months had gone by.

Then he flew in from Boston to check on me. It was just first light, and we took a break to watch the sun come up. I sat down on a rock under a palm and tried to catch my breath. There was the gentlest of tropical breezes, and some kind of colorful bird about the size of a pigeon making a racket in a coconut palm just overhead. There was a sudden movement—squawking, the flutter of wings—and he was gone.

"Palm tree python," Tiny said.

"You serious? Never seen any snakes around here," I said.

"You won't. They live high up, only species the mongoose didn't wipe out."

"Rough world out there, even here," I said.

"Law of the jungle. Speaking of which, another lobsterman tried to make a move on your traps."

"And?"

"And I let him know that wasn't a good plan. You'll have something to go back to if you don't end up killing yourself."

"There's a comfort," said.

"You got some kind of master plan in mind when you finally get your act together?"

"Work in progress," I said. "I'll keep you in the loop."

"I'm there when you need me."

"All set for now," I said.

"Whatever you need," he offered.

"Just so I can count on you to open a few doors for me."

"You can count on me for anything," Tiny said.

He stood up beside me, bent down and touched his toes. His jersey rode up, exposing the holstered nine millimeter Glock in the small of his back.

I felt something pop in my back, but it was a good pop.

"Let's get to the gym," I said. "The heavy bag's waiting on me."

TINY HIT HIS STOP WATCH and held the bag steady as I started right in, with my regular routine. I moved side to side, throwing punches, ducking and weaving; then started mixing in a few straight kicks. A couple of them forced Tiny to hang on tight. I was getting light headed, but I managed to wrap up the workout with a roundhouse kick that rattled the chain holding the bag to the ceiling.

I bent down, with my hands on my thighs, trying to get my breath.

"How … long … I go," I managed.

Tiny looked at his stop watch. "Just under six minutes—not bad."

"That's a personal best for me," I said.

"Power's coming back, too. Whacking it pretty good. You ever do one of those fancy kicks?"

"Flying roundhouse?"

"Yeah. ... Where you jump up and let her fly, regular Bruce Lee."

I caught my breath and stood up straight, stretching my back. The sweat was getting in my eyes. "Not yet. ... But give me a minute." I took a couple of really deep breaths and nodded to Tiny. He grabbed the bag and I started right in, giving it everything I had, one stiff chop right after another. The bag started to rock.

"That's more like it," Tiny said.

I started mixing straight kicks in, at first just below waist high, then mixing them up with head kicks and quick hand work.

"Looking good," Tiny said.

Sweat ran down my back, I was starting to feel lightheaded, but I kept it up. I threw a high roundhouse kick, turned and threw another from the opposite direction. The sweat was blurring my vision. I threw a rapid six-punch combination, then jumped a full two feet into the air and hit the bag with my very first flying roundhouse. It was a beaut: the bag was actually lifted right off the chain. If Tiny hadn't been hanging on it would have fallen right onto the floor.

The room started to spin. I tried to catch my breath but couldn't. I found myself on the seat of my pants and then puked all over myself. I sat there looking up at him with glassy eyes.

"How long?" I said.

"Eight big ones," Tiny said.

I wiped the puke off my chin and nodded.

I was still down and taking deep breaths.

"Hail the conquering hero."

I looked up. It was Megan, with a tall glass of lemonade in

each hand.

"Thought you were still up in Boston," I said, struggling to my feet. I wiped my mouth with the back of my hand. It was the best I could do.

"Missed you," she said, and handed Tiny his drink. We never took our eyes off each other.

She handed me mine. She handed me a towel. I cleaned myself up as well as I could, but I smelled like a goat. ... Worse, a puke goat. Tiny tossed me his Binaca breath spray. I gave myself a half dozen full blast and started to feel almost human.

I took her in my arms and held her for a very long time.

"Thought you might be through with me," I said.

We kissed. There were tears in her eyes.

"You're giving me too much credit for intelligence," she said.

"Kindred spirits."

I kissed her again.

CHAPTER 43

Tiny was down for the weekend, staying at the condo with a woman he'd brought along. Megan and I had his catamaran, *Dancer*, all to ourselves. Diehard New England sailors look down their noses at cats, not real sailboats at all. But I was coming around. She had two hulls instead of one; no heeling, fast and flat, and comfort and space off the charts. *Dancer* had three staterooms with king-sized beds, three heads and a Viking kitchen, a far cry from my old cramped space on the *Queen Anne's Revenge*. I was up early as usual; it was just after six. I poured myself a second cup of coffee. Megan joined me in the galley in her robe. She was still half-asleep. I kissed her and handed her a cup. I was in my workout shorts, getting ready to head out.

"Off to the office, dear?" she said.

"Running late," I said. "Tiny's probably already at the gym."

She sat down and sipped her coffee, noticing my Wilbur

Smith paperback, *A Time to Die*, on the table. Right next to a new pocket dictionary and a sheet of paper.

"Somehow I hate that title. It's a little too close to what happened to you. How late were you up last night?" she asked.

"Just after eleven."

She raised an eyebrow. "Late for you."

"Got into Wilbur, couldn't put him down."

"You've been doing a lot of reading down here."

"Yeah ... getting into it for some reason."

"Maybe you're growing up."

"Nah, that can't be it."

"Then what's with the dictionary?"

"Couple of words he uses a lot, didn't know what they meant."

"Really."

"Yeah, *obsequious* ... and *ubiquitous*. Looked them up and wrote them down. Figured this might be a good time to start expanding my vocabulary."

"When did this dictionary business start?"

"Since you took off on me, couple of months, I guess. Got around a hundred words on my list; put them in alphabetical order.

She smiled and picked up my notes. "You're not going to turn into an intellectual on me, are you? I don't know if I could take the shock."

"Don't laugh at me. I'm only trying to make myself worthy of you."

She looked at me, really serious.

"Never went to Harvard, this is about the best I can do."

"Sounds like you made me a regular project."

"Want to make sure you hang around a while."

"I plan to."

"Well," I said, and kissed her. She threw her arms around my neck. I kissed her again.

"I'm incredibly lucky to have you, you know that?" she said.

"Matter of opinion."

I picked up my gym bag and kissed her once more. "Got to go," I said.

She started to say something but stopped herself.

"Megan?"

"Nothing. ... It's nothing."

"Come on, it's okay."

"You're almost ready, aren't you," she said. It wasn't a question.

"Almost."

"I wish we could just stay here forever."

"We'll be back."

She looked away for a moment.

"Megan—"

She got up, turned her back on me, and opened the refrigerator door. "Let a girl get some breakfast, will you?"

I kissed her on the back of her neck.

"It'll be all right," I said.

She didn't respond at first. I kissed her again. She shrugged, not turning around. Took the milk out of the refrigerator without making eye contact.

"Just get it done," she said.

There was nothing else I could say. I let her have her breakfast in peace.

CHAPTER 44

Tiny worked the heavy bag as I skipped rope at the Mayflower Gym, St. John's answer to the famed Cronk Gym in Detroit. It was on the back side of the island, an area seldom visited by tourists and a true throw-back to the real pirates of the Caribbean. Nobody asked any questions, and if they did, sure as hell never got any answers. We talked as he worked it over.

"Megan doing okay?" he said. "Seems real quiet lately."

"Be getting back to work soon, little anxious, that's all."

"A little?"

I didn't answer, but just picked up my pace with the rope.

Tiny laughed. "Tough guy, huh?"

I shrugged. "I just need to get it over with."

He grunted a response and continued to give the heavy bag a working over. Sweat ran down his face.

The Mayflower wasn't much to look at: dark beams, a couple

of rings with local pugs going at it. The placed smelled like old socks despite the warm ocean breeze passing through. There were no walls, just a thatched roof to keep out the rain.

Hip-hop blared from a huge boom-box damned near as big as a full-sized steamer trunk. Tiny finished up on the bag with a short right hand that tore it off the chain and sent in crashing to the floor. The action in the two rings stopped as everyone looked over. Scattered applause followed. Tiny smiled and took an exaggerated bow.

The two guys in the ring we'd been waiting for finished up. We climbed under the ropes and were just about to get started with our sparring session when a kid, with a Raiders cap on sideways, came over to the ropes and leaned in. I'd seen him around, an up-and-comer, Leroy Thomas. He was at least my height, coffee complexion with just a hint of cream, shaved head, thick through the neck with bulging biceps, broad shoulders and fine chiseled features. He was a good-looking kid and he knew it.

"Hey, Pop, I been waiting for that ring," he said. Anybody over thirty was "Pop" to Leroy.

"There's a signup," I said. "Didn't see you on it."

"Don't need no signup," the kid said. "My turn," he climbed into the ring. He was in his trunks with his hands taped but he hadn't yet put on his gloves. Tiny started toward him. I saw the look in his eye and put my hand on his chest.

"Your partner here yet?" I said.

"He be here soon," the kid said, and started to dance around the ring, shadow-boxing. We'd been dismissed.

"Want to mix it up a little till he shows?" I asked.

The kid snorted but didn't bother to look my way. He threw a flurry of lightning shots at the air, then tossed off a half dozen kicks. "You don't want none of this, Pop," he said. "Full contact ... I ain't playin'."

"I'll take my chances. You okay with that, Tiny?"

"Why not?" He climbed out under the ropes, then called me over and whispered in my ear. "Don't let the fuckin' kid get ya down. ... He'll kill ya."

"Keep it in mind," I said.

The kid stood stock still and gave me his best night-train stare. He shouted to the trainer, never taking his eyes off me.

"Walter!" he shouted. "Get my gloves, Pops here wants a lesson!"

All the other action in the gym stopped. Suddenly we were the center of attention. Walter, the trainer, laced up the kid's gloves. Walter was a little fellow, with white hair and a bushy mustache. His shoulders were stooped.

"Three rounds," the kid said to the trainer. "If he last that long." He turned to the boys around the ring and smiled.

I nodded. "Seen you around," I said. "Leroy, isn't it?"

"Leroy," the kid said, and put the accent on the last syllable.

"Ah ... Leroy," I said, using the same accent he did. "*Enchante.*"

Tiny snickered on the other side of the ropes. The kid's smile disappeared. He pounded his gloves together. "Fuck you," he said.

"I'll get the head gear," the trainer said.

"Don't need no head gear. Fuck that."

"Guess I'll take a pass, too," I said.

The trainer nodded.

I smiled as he stepped outside the ropes.

"Time!" Walter shouted.

The kid moved in fast. Quick hands, he threw a six-punch combination catching me off guard for a second. Every punch was thrown with deadly intentions. He was showboating for his pals and landed a couple of solid hits. I felt a warm trickle down the side of my face. He'd opened a decent-sized cut just over my left eye. I gave him a big smile, covered up as well as I could and leaned way back into the ropes, moving my head as far away as possible. He continued with his assault, but not much got through. Finally, he stepped back and gave me room to come to the center of the ring.

"You ain't got nothing," he said.

"Yeah?"

He waved me over; I came straight ahead in a slow shuffle-step and threw a left hand he easily sidestepped. My timing just wasn't there. Sparring was one thing, but this was the real McCoy. It had been a while. He tagged me with three more quick shots before I had any idea they were coming and then tagged me with his first straight kick right between my legs. I bent over in agony. Tiny yelled and ducked under the ropes to come to my aid, stepping between the two of us.

"Foul!" Walter shouted. "You keep it clean, Leroy!"

Leroy went to his corner and grinned at his ringside pals.

"You done," Tiny said.

"Not just yet," I said. "Give me a minute." I walked around the ring trying to get it together, holding my crotch.

"Any time you ready, Pops," Leroy said. "I got lotsa more."

I chased him all around the ring, but he was a dance master.

He tagged me with a dozen more unanswered shots, and five kicks, three of which really rocked me.

"Time!" Walter shouted. We both retired to our corners and waiting stools. The kid remained standing, joking with his pals.

Tiny sponged my face and applied some Vaseline to my cut.

"Kid's too much for ya," he said. "You're not there yet."

"Nah, just getting warmed up."

"You sure?"

"I'm sure. Guy couldn't hurt me with an ax."

Tiny shook his head. "Your funeral," he said.

"Time!" Walter shouted.

I jumped off my stool and went straight at him. It was more of the same. I was a half-step behind, never getting through. He peppered me with counter-shots and targeted the cut over my eye to get it bleeding again, this time a lot worse. Half my face was covered in blood, and it was dripping down onto my chest. I pawed at it and tried to blink it away, but my vision was blurring. I looked over to my corner. Tiny had a towel in his hand, ready to throw it in.

The kid caught me with solid kick, trying to take my knee out. It was just a little low but it did wobble me. He went back upstairs with a good right hand. I tried to cover the cut over my eye and succeeded. No problem for the kid; he opened a second one over my other eye.

He taunted me. "Come on, Pop, show me something!" he shouted, and then he threw a lead right hand not bothering to set it up with a jab.

I ducked it and tagged him with a solid left to his ribs. You could hear the crack all over the gym. The kid winced and brought down his guard. I jumped up and really nailed him with a flying roundhouse kick right at the point of his jaw.

He went down hard, landing flat on his face. It was dead silence ringside. His legs twitched a couple of times. Then he lay there like someone had shot him with a gun.

I stood over him. "How was that?" I said.

Tiny came rushing over and hugged me. "You're back!" he said.

"Got a ways to go," I said. "But on my way. We have a flight to book."

CHAPTER 45

Tiny gave me a double take when I met him at the St. John airstrip. Ax just smiled.

"Morning, boys," I said.

I had on dark glasses. My head was shaved clean, my beard gone. I'd had the stylist leave me a respectable Fu Manchu mustache. Then I had him dye it jet black, along with my eyebrows. I had gold loops in both ears, twice the size of the single one I used to wear in my left.

"Jesus, wouldn't have recognized you," Tiny said.

"That's the idea." I took off my glasses and blinked in the light. I thought Tiny was going to fall off his chair. My blue eyes were dark brown, almost black.

"What the hell?"

"Contacts, going to take me a little getting used to." I tipped my head back and hit both eyes with a little Visine.

"Gonna take me a little getting used to, too," Tiny said.

"Looking good, man," Ax added.

Boston was gray when we touched down just after noon. I looked out the window as Tiny drove us up Route 1 to Marblehead. He took the Squires Road exit in Revere, by the Cinema Complex.

"You planning on catching a flick?" I said.

"Little lunch," Tiny said. "Figured we needed to talk, someplace quiet, no distractions."

I gave him a sideways look. "Very professional of you."

"Yeah. Was going to drop you off at home first, but this could be a good test."

"Test?"

"Meeting some of the boys. Let's see if anybody recognizes you."

Ax patted Tiny on the back. "A hundred says they don't."

"You're on," Tiny said, and shook on it.

He pulled into the parking lot of the Birdcage Lounge.

Hadn't been there in years, but I knew the joint well enough. The marquee read: "All Nude American College Girl Review." Babes sliding down poles. "Nice," I said. "Didn't know they served food here."

Tiny pulled into a space, turned off the engine and opened the door. "Oh, yeah, long time now. Order the Health Plate. They come from all over for the Health Plate, get it all the time." Tiny owned a major piece of the club.

He put the window down a crack and I gave the kids some dog treats. They're very forgiving if they have treats.

The bouncer greeted Tiny warmly. Tiny stuffed a twenty in the guy's breast pocket. We joined a half-dozen of his boys at a table right next to the stage. He introduced me around as Robinson Crusoe. I didn't know all of Tiny's boys well, but I did *know* them. I shook hands all around and looked every one of them right into their eyes. There was not the slightest flash of recognition. Ax held his hand out. Tiny slipped him a hundred; I passed my first big test.

Tiny hit the ATM. He took out two grand in twenties—no three-hundred-dollar limit for the big man. The dancers were on him like vultures the minute the ATM pumped out the last of the bills. Tiny ordered lunch—a fat burger, French fries and onion rings with four beers to wash it down. He wasn't fooling around. I did my soda water thing and took a pass on the chow. He dismissed his admirers for a few minutes and settled in to watch a favorite of his on stage, a tall blond with long legs and boobs that defied the laws of gravity. He stuffed a half dozen twenties in her garter belt, then turned to me.

"Nice girl," he said.

"Yeah."

We sat there for a few minutes and watched the action on stage. Finally, his lunch arrived. Tiny waited till he had his mouth full before he said a word.

We leaned our heads together and tried to make ourselves heard over the music. His boys were oblivious and otherwise occupied. We might as well have been in a soundproof booth. "So, you finally ready to let me in on your plans? Been damn close-mouthed. What ya got in mind?" Tiny said.

"What do you think? Tracking the son of a bitch down."

"You got any idea where to start?"

"Going to assume he's based here in the States," I said.

"That narrows it right down."

"You're going to help me narrow it down a hell of a lot further."

"Don't see how."

"Guy's a top-notch hit. They don't come cheap. Only so many people can afford a guy like that. Set up a meet with the boys in Rhode Island."

"Already checked that out, nothing."

"I *know* you checked it, but we need to check it again. Been a year, things might have changed."

"Maybe."

"No business ever has one hundred percent customer satisfaction. Maybe Cooney's made some enemies."

Tiny smiled. "All right, all right, I'll set it up with Michael. If anybody knows anything, it'll be him."

"That was my surmise," I said.

Tiny gave me a sideways look. "Surmise? Jesus, that woman's ruint you."

"She's doing what she can," I said. "Too bad Cooney never worked for you."

Tiny smiled. "Nah, that sort of stuff gets handled in-house."

"Figured that," I said.

"When the time comes, I want in," Tiny said.

I patted him on the shoulder. "I'll let you know when the time comes. But Cooney's mine."

"You planning on killing that guy?"

"Still on the clock."

"Damn right," Tiny said.

"Can't spring your little pal that way, can I?" I said.

"How come I only halfway believe you?" Tiny said.

"Sorry, big man."

"You got anything else you want to lay on me?" he said.

"Not at the moment."

He waved to his admirers. "Then how 'bout letting a fella enjoy the show?" He pulled out his fat wad of twenties. In a flash, Tiny was buried up to his eyeballs in boobs.

CHAPTER 46

Michael Umile runs what's left of the Patriarca crime organization from the very same office on Atwells Ave. where his great uncle, Raymond Patriarca, ran the organization during Prohibition. At one point, his family had run the whole show in New England. At that time, the Mob still owned three-quarters of the politicians, and it was unusual to find a judge anywhere in Providence who wasn't in Raymond's pocket. Raymond was an old man when I was just starting out on the force, but I knew him. Everybody knew him. Michael had always been at his side. Thanks to the Feds, RICO and wiretaps, the third generation didn't have it so good. Still, it was a big mistake to write them off.

There were a couple of toughs with slicked-back black hair and silk shirts, open at the collar, hanging out by a metal desk just off the entry. They both stood as we entered, and went for their guns. Tiny smiled and held up his hands.

"Easy, you Guidos; we're just here to see Michael," he said.

I stood with my hands in plain sight.

"My name ain't Guido," the bigger of the two said.

Tiny smiled. "I know that, Joey. He's expecting us. Do your thing."

We handed him our pistols, butt first, and the other guy patted us down.

"Who's your pal?" Joey asked.

"He's okay," Tiny said. "We're working a deal together."

"Name's Armando Lazarus," I said.

I caught Tiny giving me a look out of the corner of his eye.

Joey just made a face and motioned with his hand. "All right, ya's can go in," he said.

"Lazarus?" Tiny said on the way in.

"Couldn't help myself."

Michael was a little guy. He had a pencil-thin mustache, receding short black hair flecked with gray. He wore a blue double-breasted pinstriped suit. He was on the phone and very agitated, and didn't so much as look up as we entered. There were two ashtrays on his battered wooden desk, overflowing with butts. The guy kept us waiting a good ten minutes, pretending we weren't there. Eventually he swore, slammed down the phone and looked us over.

"So, what you want?" he said. His voice was raspy.

"Looking for a guy," Tiny said.

"Yeah?"

"A hit," I said.

Michael looked at me hard.

"Do I know this guy?" he said to Tiny.

"Nah, but I do. He's okay."

Michael checked me out a little longer, then nodded and spoke to Tiny. "Yeah, so, you got a name?"

"No."

"Good-sized guy," I said. "Six-three, six-four, Irish, looks like Gerry Cooney."

Michael shrugged. "Why come to me? Go to the fucking boys in blue, why don'tcha?"

"Yah, right," Tiny said.

"Sounds like a guy did a job for me a few years back, real pro." he said.

I leaned forward in my chair. "You have a name?"

"O'Conner," he said. "Liam O'Conner. But I don't got no idea if that's the guy's real name."

"You got any idea where he is?" I said.

Michael leaned forward and put his elbows on the table. "No idea. Hooked up with him through Frankie Cardone out in Chicago. But don't go looking to talk to Frankie; he ain't around no more."

"Dead end," Tiny said.

"You could say that, yeah," Michael said.

"You got anything else on O'Conner?" I said.

"Nothing, but you could talk to Paulie Federico. He's the guy took over for Frankie. I'll call him for ya. Ain't gonna talk to you 'less I do."

"Didn't expect you to be so helpful," Tiny said.

"You got a beef with this guy O'Conner, don'tcha?"

"I do," I said.

"Couple years after he done the job for me, he comes back. This time he's working for somebody else. Joe Romone, best man at my wedding. You remember him, Tiny?"

"Took two in the back of the head," Tiny said.

"O'Conner never cleared nothing with me first—fuckin' guy. Ain't no such thing as professional courtesy no more."

I stood up and offered Michael my hand. "No, Michael, there ain't," I agreed.

CHAPTER 47

I pushed the weight on the scale to the right at the House of Iron, in Chicago, before I got it balanced right. A kid with a shaved head and a bull neck right behind me waited his turn.

"Two-oh-eight," I said. "Good knockout weight."

The kid laughed and stepped on as I stepped off, moving the main weight over from two hundred to three hundred, then making his fine adjustment with the smaller one.

He frowned as the scale came into proper balance.

"Three fifteen," he said. "Down three."

"You're doing all right," I said, and slapped him on the back. The kid had to have had a twenty-four-inch neck.

I hit the bench, by far the smallest guy in the gym, but did fine for a welterweight. I warmed up with a single set of twelve reps at one thirty-five, jumped up to two twenty-five for three more sets of twelve, and for the grand finale, one rep with four hundred-five.

That's were the animals at the House of Iron start off to loosen up, but it's as good as a little wussie like me has ever done. I was officially back.

I was to meet Paulie Federico at three-thirty. His office was in the Sears Tower. It was a damned good-sized office on the forty-third floor. A bright-eyed brunette receptionist told me to take a seat. The waiting room was huge, but I was the only guy in it. I didn't wait long. The receptionist got the call and led me into his office.

Paulie sat behind one of those glass-and-chrome desks. Two Scandinavian leather chairs with round wooden bases faced the desk. There were great views of the city through the glass walls.

Paulie stood, offering his hand. He wasn't at all what I'd expected. He wore tan cords, soft-skinned tassel loafers, and a light blue cashmere sweater over an oxford shirt. His only jewelry was a solid gold watch—a Cartier or Pateck Philippe; I wasn't sure which. He was my height, with blue eyes and neatly-trimmed blonde hair.

"Quite a place," I said.

"Thank you, Mr. Lazarus. We have to keep up appearances. Please call me Paul, not Paulie. All right?"

"Of course," I said.

"My family was from the north of Italy, right next to Switzerland. It's a changing world." His accent was clipped and crisp, with the soft "R"s coming out "Ah." If I hadn't known better I'd have taken him for a Cabot or a Lodge.

"Used to have to be Sicilian on both sides," I said.

"That's the old days. Then it was only one side, after that, any Italian heritage at all. Now it's anybody who ever ordered spaghetti and meatballs. Have a seat."

I filled him in.

"Yes, I know him," Paul said. "Frankie used him a half-dozen times."

"He ever in your employ?" I said.

"Never saw the need. I think the late Mr. Cardone got carried away with himself."

"How so?" I said.

"O'Conner's a specialist and extremely expensive. I'd never lay out that kind of money for the people I need to go away. Now, if I needed to knock off the president, he's the very first guy I'd call," he said.

"What can you tell me about him?"

"All of his work is one hundred percent guaranteed. Never takes a dime up front and travels wherever he has to in order to get the job done. There are never any loose ends and nothing ever comes back on the man who hires him. He gets paid in cash, COD, you might say, and my understanding is it's an excellent plan to immediately live up to your end of the bargain. Once the job's done, he vanishes into thin air."

"His fee?"

"Depends on the job and the risk involved," Paul said. "Big cartel guy bought it down in Mexico. His pals didn't even begin to know where to look. He's worth whatever he asks for if the situation's right."

"He'll take any job?" I said.

"That's what I hear."

"You have any idea where he can be found?" I said.

"Last I heard, LA." Paul said. "He was living with some woman out there, actress or model, I'm not sure, but a real knockout. The way he had it set up, the only way you could contact him was through her."

"A buffer," I said.

Paul nodded.

"Her name?"

"Not a clue," Paul said.

"Do you have any contact out there who might have some information?"

"Salvatore Maranzano," he said. A smile played on the corners of his lips.

"You've got to be kidding me," I said.

He laughed. "You know your history. The original got thrown out a tenth-floor window by none other than Lucky Luciano and company."

"He's the guy thought he was Caesar, set the families up like Roman legions," I said.

"Right you are," Paul said. "Even had a bust of himself in his office. Tall, slender, elegant, *Capo di Tutti i Capi*, a regular aristocrat."

"The last boss of all bosses," I said.

"The good old days, before it all went corporate."

"They're related?" I said.

"A grand nephew," Paul said.

"His namesake cut from the same cloth?"

"Not so you'd notice," Paul said, and then laughed. "They call him Sally Clams. Guy's a classic. I'll let him know you're coming."

"I'll look forward to meeting Mr. Clams. Anything else you can tell me?"

"As a matter of fact, yes. I know Michael has a problem with this guy. I'm sure you have your reasons, too, but it's a stupid play. Too damned dangerous. Let it go."

"Sorry," I said.

"Pity," Paul said. "I wish I could root for you."

"You can't?" I said.

Paul smiled. "I'm a businessman. Never know, one of these days I just might want to knock off a president."

CHAPTER 48

The message light was blinking on the phone in my hotel room when I got back from my meeting with Paul. It was from Tiny, and marked urgent. I called him right back, catching him on his cell.

"What's up?" I asked.

"Got a small problem with our boy," he said.

"What boy's that?"

"Shawn Corbett, what other boy we got?"

"Right, right," I said. "Almost forgot all about him."

"I haven't. Kid got in a knife fight. Mother's going nuts."

"He dead?" I said.

"Nah, but the other guy's in critical condition."

"They have him in solitary, don't they?" I said.

"Yeah."

"So what's the problem? Not like he can get into a whole lot of grief in there."

"Listen, Fenway ... the kid's losing it, no telling what he might end up doing."

"Not my problem," I said.

There was a long silence on the line. "You still there?" I said.

"Fenway ... the kid's my brother."

"Your what?"

"Half-brother. Old man had the wandering eye; didn't know myself 'til a year ago, told me on his deathbed. He made me promise I'd look out for him."

"Your mother know about any of this?" I said.

"Nothing, and I want to keep it that way."

"Explains a lot."

"Shouldn't have kept it from you."

"Doesn't make any difference now. Look, just tell the kid there are things in the works, but he's got to keep his nose clean or it's all out the window."

"Don't know if he'll buy it," Tiny said.

"He's got no choice, does he? He kills someone on the inside, won't make any difference what we come up with."

"Right," Tiny said.

MY NEXT CALL WAS TO CAPTAIN MERRITT back in Boston. I filled him in on my progress in tracking down Liam O'Conner, AKA Cooney.

"So what can I do for you?" Merritt said.

"I've got a name for you now; issue a warrant for his arrest for murder and attempted murder, and let the LA cops know I'm working with you."

"Done," Merritt said. "Got a contact guy out there for you, Captain Hector Gonzales, good man."

"Just so I'm covered," I said.

"They'll know you're working with us. I'll put it in writing," Merritt said. "But watch your ass. You've got some slack with the LAPD, but for the love of God, don't go shooting up any civilians."

"Don't plan to."

"Media comes down on ya, won't make any difference who you're working with."

"Got no desire to get my picture in the papers."

"You got plenty to deal with as it is. You figure you can put the collar on him on your own?"

"Got to find him first."

"Yeah, yeah," Merritt said.

"What's going on with Quinn and internal affairs?"

"Not enough to spring Corbett, if that's what you mean," Merritt said.

"You know Quinn set him up."

"I got nothing," Merritt said.

"Nothing at all on Quinn's computer?"

"Zip," Merritt said. Been two years, hard drive's been cleared."

"There's got to be something; another hard drive in a recycle box, maybe. Nothing ever really disappears."

"Checked and rechecked."

"That's terrific."

"It's the way it is. Quinn had an unblemished record for twenty-five years. You want me to tell the DA to call a hearing because some private dick's got suspicions?"

"And the coroner," I added. "He thinks it was possible for Mark Sullivan to break his own neck?"

"He agreed with you; not likely, but possible," Merritt said. "Anyway, the cameras were down, you know that."

"Any prints from where the wires were cut?"

"Squat."

"Perfect."

"You want to put a wrap on this, we got to have Cooney or O'Conner, whatever the hell his name is," Merritt said. "Simple as that."

I hung up. It was time to point Tiny's private jet at LA.

CHAPTER 49

I stopped in to see Hector Gonzales of the LAPD. He was short but thick, not quite going to pot but getting there. He had a full head of brown hair combed straight back, with a bushy mustache.

He kept me waiting about half an hour, then came out of his office and waved me in. He spoke to me over his shoulder as he walked.

"Zoo here today," he said. "You're Merritt's guy, right?"

"Right."

He closed the door to his office, took a seat behind his desk and pointed to one of the leather chairs facing him. "Got some paperwork," he said, then handed me a stack of forms on a clipboard. "Fill those out while I make a copy of your badge."

I hesitated a second, then handed it over. He glanced at it as he stood up, then stopped short. Just under my number, all in caps: RETIRED.

"Merritt didn't tell me you were no longer on the force," Gonzales said.

"Just a technicality," I said.

"Yeah, right. Fill out the forms. I gotta make a phone call."

I waited close to an hour before he came back. He handed me two more forms and told me to sign off. "As of right now, you're a special deputy with the LAPD."

"Didn't know you guys had deputies."

"That's what they're calling you anyway; new one on me," he said.

I gave him my best smile. I thought for sure I was going to get some grief.

"Do I have to take an oath?" I said.

"Fuck you think this is? Dodge City?"

🔫 🔫 🔫

I CHECKED INTO THE HOTEL and then kept my appointment with Mr. Clams. Sally didn't bother to stand as I entered our private room at DeLuca's, just off Rodeo Drive. The room had an ornate crystal chandelier. The paneling was cherry and trimmed with blue velvet wallpaper. Sally was Paul's opposite number; built like a pork barrel, he sat at the head of a long table with a crisp white tablecloth and two candelabras. He held a pasta spoon in one hand, fork in the other. There were spots of tomato sauce on his white shirt and blue silk tie.

Sally had a comb over that would put Donald Trump to shame, dyed jet black. A huge underbite gave him a bulldog look: lower teeth prominent, uppers invisible. Paul hadn't been kidding;

this guy was a classic. Everything about him screamed Mafia, from tailored sharkskin suit to pinky ring and a diamond-encrusted watch that caught the overhead light and lit up the room like one of those old mirrored balls you used to see hanging from dance hall ceilings.

Sally Clams had three chins, and weighed three hundred pounds if he weighed an ounce. They told me I'd need a jacket to get in. I wore my blue double-breasted Brooks Brothers blazer with white linen slacks. I packed a bow tie, but didn't bother wearing it.

The two thick-necked mutts sitting with him were stuffed into suits that looked two sizes too small. They stood up and patted me down. "He's clean, Boss," the bigger of the two announced.

I took a seat. Sally looked me up and down. "No fuckin' way you're in Michael's crew," he said.

"I'm not."

"Then what the fuck you doin' here?"

"My goals and his are not dissimilar."

Sally just sat there looking at me, then broke out laughing. "Paulie told me you was a wise guy," he said.

"He tell you anything else?" I said.

"Said you was working with Umile, trying to find a guy."

"You'll help?" I asked.

"Forgetaboutit, Michael and I go back a long ways. Used to get up to Providence all the time. I'm from New York."

"No fooling," I said.

He started to answer, and then stopped himself. He gave me a look. "Who you looking for?" he said.

"A hit, expensive one, name's Liam O'Conner," I said. "You know him?"

Sally looked to his two associates, then back to me. "You got a job for him?" he said. "I ain't got no beef with Umile."

I waved him off. "And Michael's got no beef with you. We just have a little unfinished business, that's all."

"Just so this guy don't come after me." Sally said.

"Not why I'm here," I said, and looked him right in the eye. "You going to help me or what?"

A waiter opened the door and came in carrying a tray, interrupting us. It was the main course. He placed an enormous platter of pasta in front of Sally, with a three-pound-plus whole lobster right on top. For a second there I thought Sally forgot I was in the room. The waiter served the other two men and turned to me.

"Anything for you, sir?"

"I—"

Sally cut me off. "Bring him the Lobster Fra Diablo," Sally said, to me: "You gotta try it."

I looked at the menu. "Tell you the truth, I was thinking of the veal," I said.

Sally's eyes turned to two cold black stones. "You trying to piss me off. Fuck's wrong wit' you?"

I held up both my hands and smiled. "No sir, no problem at all," I said.

Sally gave me another look, but then lightened when I place my order. "Wait 'til you try it," he said.

I was back in his good graces.

I REGISTERED AT THE WILSHIRE and unpacked my Hartman bag,

then put my clothes neatly in the bureau drawers. I didn't plan to live out of a suitcase—had a feeling I was going to be around a while.

There was a UPS Ground package waiting for me at the hotel. I unwrapped the metal carrying case and placed it on the bed. Inside: all my old pals—two, nine millimeter Glocks and two Mac 10 automatic machine pistols with enough ammo to storm Fort Knox. I changed into jeans and a sweatshirt, then called the front desk and made arrangements for a rental car.

I took off for the desert. Three hours later I was in the middle of nowhere. I pulled off on a dirt road, set up some targets and let fly. I made a couple of minor adjustments and was good to go.

When I got back to the hotel, there was a message from Sally, telling me to expect a call. I didn't have long to wait; a Miss Crystal Bates said I was to meet her the following morning in the hotel restaurant.

"How will I know you?" I said.

"You won't have to," she said. "I'll know you. Eight o'clock." The phone went dead.

CHAPTER 50

I wore a flowered tropical shirt, open at the collar, cargo pants, and boat shoes. I showed up a half-hour early, sipped coffee and opened up my laptop. I used Armando Lazarus's new password and Googled my breakfast companion. A California blonde, she had her own web site and a fair number of movies to her credit: *Back Seat Cabby, Teach Me How to Do It, Boff Along Cassidy* and *Log Jam.* Just enter your credit card and you could download the lot. *Ah, yes, another Hollywood success story.*

"Doing a little research?" she asked, taking the seat across from me.

I looked up. Her website didn't do her justice. She had delicate features with full lips and high cheekbones. Long, natural blonde hair framed intelligent blue eyes. She wore a light gray Chanel suit with a stylishly short skirt. She'd gone a little overboard with the silicone, but I was willing to overlook it.

"Just killing time," I said. "You were running a little late."

She smiled and poured herself a cup of coffee from the silver pitcher on the table, then picked up the menu.

"Late night," she said. The waiter came over. "Just the fruit cup."

I was halfway through with my eggs Benedict.

She watched the waiter's back and spoke when he was too far away to hear.

"Did Mr. Moranzano explain the terms?" she asked.

"No."

"It's cash only. You'll speak to Mr. O'Conner directly as to the actual amount, but I can tell you in advance that he demands an extremely high premium. Is that a problem?"

"Not if he's as good as advertised," I said, just before the waiter arrived with her fruit cup.

"He is," she said, once he left us alone. "Do you mind if I ask you a few questions?"

"You can ask."

"Where is the job?"

"Costa Rica."

"Is the person in question a member of one of the cartels?"

I shook my head. "We're having some labor troubles."

"Union busting," she said.

"You could say that," I said.

"And you're not in a position to take care of the matter with the resources you have on hand?"

"The matter requires the utmost discretion," I said.

"You can't afford recriminations?" she said.

I smiled. "You've found me out."

"The person's name?"

"I'll share that with the contractor directly. Are you acquainted with the nature of Mr. O'Conner's work?"

"He describes himself as a facilitator. I'm not privy to his methods, only that there are never any complaints."

"So, you know nothing," I said.

"Only what I told you," she said. "I'm paid to ask you the questions, Mr. Lazarus."

"I see."

"What's the name of your company?"

I just shook my head.

She smiled.

"As I said, you can ask."

"Is Armando Lazarus your real name?"

"Crystal Bates yours?"

"Fair enough," she said. "You came well recommended."

"When can I expect to hear from your Mr. O'Conner?"

"You can expect a call here at the hotel in a couple of days, maybe three. He's out of town." She got up. "Oh, in case you're not aware, we're being watched."

"I assumed so."

"I'm not to be followed, is my point."

"Of course."

"Trust me. They'll pick up any tail in an instant."

"Assumed that, too."

CHAPTER 53

Tiny and company checked into a nondescript hotel just outside of LA. I kept myself busy at the hotel gym. It wasn't until day four that I finally got the call. It was just before five p.m.

"Mr. Lazarus, I understand you're expecting to hear from me," he said.

"I am." I felt my heart skip a beat, but kept my cool.

There was a silence for a moment.

"Palo Alto and Vine, there's a parking garage. You can't miss it. Go to the top floor and park in number three-twenty-five at seven tonight," he said. His Irish accent was almost completely gone, but it was unmistakably O'Conner.

"Got it," I said.

"You're to come alone. Is that clear?"

"It's clear."

"Don't keep me waiting." The phone went dead.

I called Tiny on a new encrypted cell with no GPS chip, on the off-chance that somehow O'Conner was onto my regular phone.

MY MOUTH GREW DRY, and my palms began sweating. I put on my lightweight Kevlar body armor and did my stretching routine down on the floor, methodically pulling back one leg and then the other. I did a hundred crunches and stretched some more, losing myself in the familiar routine. I felt myself calming down.

I stood in front of the mirror and stretched my arms straight out with my palms down, steady as a rock. I smiled at my reflection, strapped on both holsters and my ammo belt, checked the actions of the Glocks and the machine pistols, grabbed a dozen clips along with the machine pistols and put them on the belt. I topped it off with a white XXL windbreaker as a cover up. There was just the slightest bulge, not at all noticeable. I didn't bother with the contact lenses. They had to be extra thick to change my eye color. I never had gotten used to them and could only wear them for a short time before my eyes started to water. That was one little distraction I could do without. It was time to go.

I hit the cross-town traffic I was expecting and turned on the radio, moving less than sixty feet in twenty minutes. My palms were still sweaty. I looked at my watch and took a deep breath. I had all the time in the world. The rental car had Sirius satellite radio. I turned to channel seventy-three, the Spa Channel, low-key music you hear in the background at the fancier spas, real Zen stuff. I laughed at myself, but it helped.

I took my ticket at the gate and drove to the roof. I backed into the space, nose-out, then shut off the ignition and looked all around. I pulled a Chicago Cubs baseball cap down tight over my forehead, covering as much of my face as I could. I didn't see anybody or any surveillance cameras—not that it made much difference. I took a seat on the front bumper of the Lincoln and waited.

I was there a full half-hour. I'd lost the jitters completely, but my mind was racing. Images from my childhood, my mother, my father, crazy things I hadn't thought of in years—the schoolyard bully, the nun who kept me after class, Whiff buying me an ice cream cone, Tiny, Megan. I was all over the map.

I heard a car come around the corner and looked up. My watch said seven on the dot. It was a late-model, black Mercedes. It parked a couple of dozen spaces away. The doors opened. The three men that got out were dressed all in black: O'Conner, a shaved-head white boy, and a black man with corn-rows bringing up the rear. O'Conner's men were both good-sized guys.

I waved them on. They never acknowledged me but came ahead. I watched them getting closer and closer and when they were just where I wanted them, I pulled out both machine pistols and jumped behind my car. They pulled theirs every bit as quick. It was a standoff.

"You're done, O'Conner. Half-a-dozen guns aimed right at your head. Drop 'em."

His henchmen looked all around. O'Conner never took his eyes off me. We still stood there, guns drawn.

"Come on, O'Conner, it's over."

"How do I know you're not alone?" O'Conner said.

"Because I have no desire to commit suicide."

"Who are you?"

"A dead man. ... Now drop 'em."

O'Conner smiled, feinted left, then dived to his right and let off three quick rounds. All hell broke loose. I missed O'Conner but caught the shaved head in the throat. He slammed up against a parked car and slowly went down clutching his neck. Blood gushed out between his fingers.

I took cover behind my Lincoln and nearly got my head shot off by a roof-top sniper a couple of buildings over. I just caught a glimpse of him as he went down from one of Tiny's boys on the building right next to it. Then I saw Ax take one and go down hard.

Fire erupted from roof-top to roof-top, like some kind of second front. They were too far away for me to get a clear shot, so I concentrated on trying to keep O'Conner's head down and maybe doing some damage.

Corn-row made an end run on me and let loose with a long burst before taking cover behind the wheel well of a white Mercedes right next to me. He jumped up and emptied both of his machine pistols, peppering the Lincoln with holes. I fired back and moved from the front to the rear wheel well, trying both to keep my head down and get a better angle.

There was no fire at all from O'Conner. I hoped to God he hadn't slipped under my radar somehow and was looking to flank me. I tried to take a quick look for him and felt a dull thud high in the chest spinning me around to the right. I hit the concrete and smacked the back of my head as I went down. Corn-row was on me in an instant. He rushed around the front end of the Lincoln, both guns blazing. Concrete dust flew up all around me. I fired from where I was and took the top of his head off. Just as I got to my feet, there was a rapid burst from behind me. With a sudden whoosh the Lincoln's gas tank went up.

The explosion knocked me off my feet. The heat was intense. O'Conner came out of nowhere. We both fired at the same time. He caught me just off center in my throat. I took out his kneecap. He screamed and went down. Blood gushed out of the side of my neck and suddenly I was both dizzy and nauseous. But I could move and with his knee gone, he couldn't.

I jumped on top of him and took away his gun before he knew what was happening. I sat on his chest holding both of his arms back with my full body weight. I could hear sirens in the background getting closer. The shooting on the roof-tops had stopped.

Our faces were less than a foot apart. We looked right into each other's eyes.

"You!" he said. *"You."*

He twisted around, getting one hand free, pulled out a short knife and jammed it all the way through my left arm.

I smashed his face with a piston blow that collapsed his cheekbone. He still hung on tight.

"Yeah," I said. "It's me, you son of a bitch. I smashed him again and he went limp. I yanked out the knife and felt my gorge rise. Then I puked all over myself. The garage started to spin. I heard shouts; Tiny and his boys would be with me any second. I raised my fist to hit him again but stopped myself.

O'Conner was no good to me dead.

CHAPTER 52

I hurt all over and it took a while for my eyes to focus. Tiny was in a folding chair opposite my hospital bed, reading a magazine. I had a tube in my arm attached to a bottle with clear liquid hanging form a metal stand. My face felt moist.

Tiny put down his magazine and smiled. "This is getting monotonous," he said.

"Ax make it? I saw him go down."

"Intensive care, touch and go. I got my money on him, though."

"O'Conner?"

"Looks a hell of a lot better than you do," Tiny said. "You're a Goddamn mess. He's in the infirmary at the lockup. He ain't going nowhere. Must have thirty cops on him; FBI and ATF boys all over the place, too."

I touched my face. There was some kind of a heavy cream

smeared all over it. "What the hell?"

Tiny laughed and handed me a mirror. "Little too close to the fire."

I took the mirror. I looked like I'd fallen asleep under a sunlamp. My face was beet red, peeling and covered with oozing open sores. My lips were cracked. The right side of my face looked like I got hit with a baseball bat.

"Jesus," I said.

Tiny got up and took my Kevlar vest off a hook on the back of the door and then handed it to me. "Three hits," he said.

"Never leave home without it," I said.

"Yeah, right. Lot of people want to talk to you," Tiny said. "Gonzales was by, so were the Feds. Merritt's on his way from Boston."

"Feds?" I said. "They going to give me a hard time?"

"Got me, but you're all set with the LAPD."

"Feds might be another matter," I said.

Tiny shook his head. "Four guys dead. Three of them had Federal warrants," he said.

"Nothing on O'Conner?" I said.

"Nothing," Tiny said.

"Feds question you yet?" I said.

"Hell no, why would they? We weren't there," Tiny said.

We both looked to the door as one of Tiny's boys came in with a copy of the *LA Times* and tossed it on the bed.

"Interesting reading," he said, and left.

I glanced at the headlines:

"FBI & LAPD IN SHOOT-OUT WITH FUGITIVES,

FOUR DEAD"

There were photos of the scene but no mention of Armando Lazarus or Fenway Burke.

"Looks like I wasn't there either," I said.

"Guess not, nothing in the papers. You ain't complaining are ya?" Tiny said.

"Hell no, long as they leave me alone." I scanned the article. "How long they going to keep me here?" I said.

"Couple more days, just to be safe," Tiny said.

"Got to have a little chat with O'Conner."

"You know where to find him."

There was a knock on the door and Megan came in. She stood there frozen, looking at me.

I gave her my best smile. My lips cracked. I felt a trickle of blood on my chin.

No response.

"Looks a lot worse than it is," I said.

"Is it over?" she said.

There was a long silence. Her eyes filled.

"The worst of it is, yes," I said.

Tears ran down her cheeks. She started to say something but she lost it.

"Megan—"

"Oh, just shut up, will you?" She rushed over to my bed, hugged me for all she was worth and started to cry.

Tiny got up and headed for the door. "Three's a crowd," he said.

"Tiny."

He turned and looked back.

"Thanks."

He smiled and left us alone.

CHAPTER 53

The Feds interviewed me bedside and really gave me a working over, but in the end I was in the clear, as long as I kept my mouth shut. Once the hospital gave me my release, I headed right for the infirmary at the lockup.

There were LAPD uniformed cops everywhere and almost as many Feds. They weren't taking any chances. I was expected. They let me in with a nod. Nobody said a word.

O'Conner had a five-day growth. There were flecks of gray in his dark brown beard. He was heavily bandaged and had a ravaged look. His right leg was elevated. His eyes were dull, either from the drugs or the situation. Either way, he was down.

I took a seat next to him and looked him in the eye.

"You know me, don't you?"

He nodded. "I do," he said. His voice was deep and strong, belying his appearance. "Lazarus ... should have put that together."

"Maybe, but it's been close to a year so that's a real reach. Doesn't make any difference now, you're bagged."

"Things change," he said.

"Not for you."

We looked at each other for a long minute.

O'Conner broke the silence. "I suppose I had to take a fall sometime, but I never saw this one coming," he said.

I shrugged.

"You didn't come here just to crow. What do you want?"

"The name of the guy who hired you," I said.

O'Conner leaned his head back on the pillow and closed his eyes. "And just why would I want to give you that?"

"Because you have no criminal record, and I'm the only witness on that day out on the water," I said. "Without my testimony they've got nothing on you, do they?"

He lifted his head off the pillow and opened his eyes. "Deal? You want to *deal*?" he said.

"I do."

"Full of surprises, you are," O'Conner said.

There was another long silence.

"I cooperate, you get amnesia?"

"It's the only play you have."

"I almost put you in your grave and killed a man who was like a father to you. You telling me you won't testify?"

"I am," I said.

O'Conner looked me right in the eye for the longest time.

"Why should I trust you?" he said.

"Because I'm telling you, you can," I said.

"True professional," O'Conner said.

I kept my mouth shut.

"There's the small matter of the shootout at the garage," O'Conner said.

"Once again, it all hinges on my testimony. You might have been an innocent bystander," I said.

"They know differently," he said.

"They know squat," I said. "But it doesn't make any difference what they think they know. They've got to prove it."

O'Conner nodded.

"You're going to have to testify against Rogers," I said.

"And incriminate myself?" O'Conner said.

"You only have to say that he contacted you to do the job, not that you took it." He just lay there, his eyes boring into mine.

"Use your head. It's your only play," I said.

"I've never given anybody up in my life."

"First time for everything. You think he'd take a fall for you if the tables were turned?"

"I don't see that happening," he said.

"So?"

"So, you expect me to rat and then fade into the woodwork?"

"You see any other options?"

He leaned his head back on the pillow and closed his eyes again. "What about our little score?"

"You don't bother me, I don't bother you," I said.

He closed his eyes again.

"I never meant to hurt the old man; he just got in the way."

"I know that. That's the one and only reason you're not dead."

"Ahh ... maybe you're not quite the professional I thought you were."

"I'm human," I said.

"Right."

I stood up. "We have a deal or not?"

He didn't hesitate. "Rogers," he said. "Rogers was the one."

"The old man or the kid?"

"Never dealt with either one of them directly," O'Conner said.

"Unusual, isn't it? You holding anything back on me?" I said.

"Not so unusual, and no, all handled through an old IRA contact. I got paid, that's all I cared about."

"Your contact verify it was Rogers?"

"He'll verify anything I tell him to, long as his ass isn't on the line."

I thought about it for a minute.

"Whoever it was, he had some dough," O'Conner said. "He paid in cash, three times the usual rate."

"I put money in your pocket," I said.

"You proved to be an expensive complication for Mr. Rogers."

"And getting more costly every day."

"That's the truth, boyo." O'Conner said. His Irish brogue suddenly reappeared.

"You sure you're not holding back. All bets are off if you are," I said.

"Why would I?"

"Why would you, indeed."

CHAPTER 54

Tiny picked Megan and me up at Logan Airport. The weather was clear but there was still a nip in the air; true summer never comes early in Boston. Bit of a shock to my system.

Tiny threw my bag in the trunk of his Maserati and headed out, instantly hitting traffic. There was some construction going on, something we'd learned to live with since the Big Dig, but still a major pain.

"So, what now?" he said.

"Can't very well ask Megan to move in unless I have a place to live," I said.

"Well, now, that is a development. You sure you don't want to think that one over, Megan?" Tiny said.

"Thanks a lot, big man," I said.

Megan smiled and gave me a kiss. "I'm sure," she said.

"Thought you'd be right back at Rogers," Tiny said.

"Got to get my feet on the ground first."

"Right, got a real estate guy for ya. You planning on staying in Marblehead?"

"What I need is a boat guy. Take me to Tommy Cloutman. You know him, don't you?"

"'T'? Sure, good man," Tiny said.

TOMMY WAS IN COVERALLS, with a short salt-and-pepper beard and a round face. He had the hands of a workman. His main business was boat maintenance, not sales, but he did have some nice ones in his yard on consignment. I introduced Megan.

He wanted to show us a Hinckley he'd just gotten in, a real beaut. She was a forty-eight-footer, dark blue with a pristine teak deck. Built in Maine for rough weather—a real New England cruiser. But the islands had done a job on me. There was a catamaran in the yard, a fifty-six-foot Privilege, all white with teak trim. I walked right over to her and pointed.

"That's the one for us, 'T,'" I said.

"A multi-hull?" Tommy said.

"Yep," I said.

"She's a honey all right; three staterooms, all with king-sized berths, Viking galley, air conditioning, premium sound system, eighty-inch plasma TVs, GPS, all finished off in teak."

"Right. Tiny's got one just like her down the islands," I said.

"She ain't no sail boat, more like some kind of a floating condo."

"Got sails, doesn't she?"

"Give you that," Tommy said.

"Then she's a damned sailboat, far as I'm concerned," I said. "You like her, Megan?"

"What's not to like?" she said, and nuzzled me.

Tommy shook his head and made a face. "I hate ta see a young fella go wrong," he said.

"Well, you know—"

He cut me off. "Damn thing'll cost ya a million bucks. You got that kinda dough lying around?"

"I got it covered," I said.

There was lettering on both sides and on the transom: *The Maryellen*, it said.

"Need to rename her," I told him.

"Bad luck to rename her."

"Can't be helped," I said.

"What ya got in mind?"

"*Whiffersnapper*," I said, and turned to Megan. "He's the guy footed the bill for all this. The name okay with you?"

"Wouldn't have it any other way," she said.

Tommy looked at me for a minute, and then smiled.

"*Whiffersnapper* it is," he said.

"We want her in the water right away."

Tommy waved to one of the crane operators and pointed to the cat. The operator jumped up on the crane and fired her up.

"That quick enough for you?" he asked.

I smiled and tossed our bags up on the deck.

CHAPTER 55

The cab dropped us off. The sign read, "Cars of Yesterday," and the place was just opening. I was there to pick up my little Porsche. A big guy with grease under his fingernails in a tattered Red Sox cap greeted Megan and me at the door.

"Here for the Speedster," I said.

He shook my hand. "Bob Ballenger."

"Fenway Burke," I said. "My girlfriend, Megan Griffin."

"Pleased to meet you both. Been wondering when you'd show up. Had the car in storage after we finally got her done. Your pal Tiny was by a half a dozen times."

"How's she looking?"

"See for yourself. I'll bring her around." He disappeared through a door and then pulled the Porsche around front. I almost didn't recognize her. She looked fresh off the assembly line. She used to be steel gray, but no more: fire engine red and gold trim, including all four exhaust pipes. The leather seats were flawless, as was the matching, tan cloth top. The BBS racing wheels had gold, magnesium centers and silver rims; tires were BF Goodrich asymmetrical comps.

She sat there idling. There was a throaty roar as he raced the engine, and then he jumped out, smiling, and held the door for me.

"The big man approved the color change," he said. "Hope it's okay."

"You kidding?" I said, and clapped him on the back. "Brand new engine?"

Megan ran her hand over the hood, looked up at me and smiled.

"Right from the Porsche factory. The old one was cooked, cracked right down the middle. These things ain't built to have a building fall on them."

I popped the hood. She had a TPC supercharger that alone must have cost over ten grand. "That ought to help," I said.

"Lot more pep," Bob agreed.

I reached for my wallet.

"Tiny's got you covered; no charge."

"Must have cost a lot more than your walkin' around cash," I ventured.

"It wasn't cheap. Enjoy." Bob headed back into the garage and left me with my new toy.

Megan hopped in. I admired the car for a moment, then ran my hand across the hood—not a flaw anywhere.

"I'll take good care of you, girl," I said, then jumped in next to Megan and roared off. I yelled to be heard over the engine noise.

"Got to shake things up a bit; how 'bout I drop you off at the boat and catch you later for lunch?"

"Maddie's?"

"I was thinking maybe head on up to Rockport. Stretch her legs a little. Something on the water."

She leaned over and kissed me. "You're on."

It was turning into a good day, and I got another kiss when I dropped Megan off. But I had a visit to make.

I kept the top down, enjoying the feel of the wind rushing through my newly close-cropped hair. There wasn't a lot of traffic. I took Route 128 south and opened her up. She effortlessly hit one-twenty. I chopped her back to eighty-five and hit the Route 9 exit for Newton, Wellesley.

ρ   ρ   ρ

I RAPPED ON RANDY ROGERS' DOOR. Nothing. I hammered away again, this time really getting into it.

"All right! All right! Take it easy, I'm coming!"

The door flew open. He was in the same silk robe he'd been wearing the last time I came by.

"Who do you—" His words trailed off.

"Morning, Randy," I said, then pushed him aside and walked right in. I took a seat on one of the leather couches just off the foyer.

"Sit down, we have a lot to talk about," I said.

He was still standing at the door. His chin just about rested on his chest.

"I thought you were dead," he said.

"Nah, just on vacation."

He came over and sat opposite me.

"What?" I said. "You're not going to offer me coffee?"

He seemed too stunned to speak.

"Your boy, O'Conner, or whatever his real name is, he's in custody."

"I don't know any such person," he said.

"Good answer," I said. "But it won't wash. You guys paid him handsomely to do a job for you. He'll give you up to save his own skin."

No response. He was having a hard time keeping it together.

"Well?"

He came out of it enough to respond, but he still wasn't all there.

"I don't know anything about it."

"Yeah, right. Listen, kid, listen carefully. It's over. The guy's going to testify. The only thing that remains a question is why you hired him. I figure you killed Simpson, then went to your old man to cover it up. He hired O'Conner when things started to unravel."

He stared at me, his eyes suddenly glassy.

"Why did you kill him?" I asked.

"I ... "

"Why?"

The kid stood up on unsteady legs. "I can't talk about this," he said. He turned his back on me and headed toward the kitchen.

"I'm afraid that's not an option, Randy. Give my regards to your old man. I'll be back."

I showed myself out. I could have popped in on his father just as easily. But it was easier to stir the pot with the weakest link. I had a feeling the old man was going to get an early-morning phone call.

CHAPTER 56

There was a formal meeting set at the DA's office with William Randal, Randy Rogers, their lawyer, Captain Merritt and me. I was in the lobby of the DA's office when Merritt rushed in, startling me.

"We got a problem," he said.

"Yeah?" I said.

"They're tearing their hair out in LA. Your prime witness has escaped."

"That's nuts. They must have had fifty guys on him. There were Feds crawling all over the place."

"Guy's got a whole organization behind him."

"Doesn't make any sense," I said. "We had a deal, and anyway, they had nothing on him. He had nothing to gain by running." I said.

"Yeah, yeah, FBI's got nothing on him, clean with Interpol,

too. But it turns out the CIA wants to talk with him, and MI-5."

"British Intelligence," I said.

"No one's saying anything, but they call him a 'person of extreme interest.' Apparently he saw it coming and hit the bricks," Merritt said.

"Jesus, how the hell did he get away? He was in traction, for Christ's sake."

"They were transporting him to a more secure facility. He overpowered his guard and a dozen guys in stocking-cap masks showed up shooting—five guards down. They took off through alleys on motorcycles. Five oil tanker-trucks blocked all the access roads when they tried to give chase. And get this: they abandon them with the valves jammed wide open. Dumped something like a hundred thousand gallons of diesel per truck, turned the roads into regular skating rinks. EPA's been called in, diesel in the storm drains; it's a regular freaking Exxon Valdese. Going to take them months to clean it up."

"EPA, huh? That'll put the fear of God in them."

"Yeah, right, traffic was backed up for miles. Looks like they disabled a couple of drawbridges for good measure, but they're still checking that one out."

"Delightful," I said.

"It's got old school IRA written all over it, and those boys know what they're doing."

"Ought to—been at it since 1166."

"Right."

"The Fed's got nothing?" I said.

"Going building to building, but nothing yet."

I let it sink in.

"There goes your case," Merritt said.

"Does the Rogers clan know anything about this?"

"Not unless the DA let them in on it, and that's not too damn likely," Merritt said.

"Then it never happened," I said, and took him by the arm. "Let's get going. We have a meeting to get to."

☞ ☞ ☞

GWEN STEWART IS AN UNLIKELY-LOOKING DA. Just over five feet tall; she has short red hair and leans to the chunky side. She wore a conservative gray suit and looked more like a librarian than a hard-driving prosecutor. But she has bulldog tenacity and graduated at the top of her class at the Harvard Law School. She came to her feet as we arrived and shook my hand with a grip that would have put any one of the Chicago Bears to shame.

"I've heard a lot about you, Mr. Burke," she said.

"And I you."

"This is your show, Mr. Burke. If there was a miscarriage of justice, it occurred under a previous administration." She pointed to a chair at the conference table. "Have a seat."

Both the Rogers and their lawyer were already seated. The Rogers were in casual attire, as if on their way to a ball game. Their white-haired lawyer wore a gray, pinstriped suit. Charles Whittaker was his name. He looked like they'd picked him up at central casting. Merritt took the chair next to mine, and the DA went to the head of the table. She introduced us all around as a stenographer came in and sat beside her.

"I thought this was an informal proceeding," Whittaker said.

"Then you were misinformed," Stewart replied.

Whittaker turned to his clients. "I must advise you to say absolutely nothing without first conferring with me." Both of the Rogers nodded, and the old man smiled.

Stewart turned to me. "So, Mr. Burke, what do you have for us today?"

"There's been a cover-up with a lot of innocent people who ended up dead," I said.

"Ah." Whittaker put in. "A conspiracy theory, how novel."

"May I continue?" I said.

"Kindly reserve your comments until Mr. Burke has told us his entire story," Stewart said.

Whittaker shook his head and frowned in his best lawyerly manner. "Story indeed," he said.

"Mr. Whittaker, you will wait your turn. Understood?"

Whittaker nodded, duly chastised.

She gave me the nod.

"Randy here killed Simpson," I said. "I don't know why, but he did."

Randy jumped up out of his chair. "That's a lie!" he shouted.

Both Whittaker and his father got him to sit down.

"Detective Quinn of the Lynn police force was bought off to pin blame on an innocent man."

"I'd hardly call Mr. Shawn Corbett an innocent man," Whittaker said.

"Mr. Whittaker," Stewart said.

Whittaker held up his hands.

"Proceed, Mr. Burke," she said.

"Innocent of this crime," I said. "I was hired by a friend of the accused man's family to get to the bottom of it all. I was warned to back off and didn't. That's when the bodies started to pile up."

Randy broke out in a sweat and started to shake. It looked like he was having some kind of fit.

"A professional hit man was hired, one Liam O'Conner. Anybody having any connection to the case got knocked off. First the bad cop, then the witnesses. More than one attempt was made on my own life. I narrowly escaped. The hit man has been brought to justice and has agreed to testify."

Nobody said a word.

"What was it, Randy? A lover's quarrel?" I said.

Randy's lower lip trembled and his eyes filled. "I never killed him," he said. "I loved him."

His father turned to him. "Shut up," he said, and made a move to strike him. Whittaker restrained him. Randy cowered and began to cry. He spoke through his tears and runny nose.

"I paid off Quinn. I admit it," he said.

"Shut up, I told you!" His old man shouted.

"But you didn't kill him?" I said.

"No ... I ... We had a big fight the night he was killed," Randy said.

"At the Other Side?" I said.

He nodded. Merritt handed him a handkerchief. "A lot of people saw it. I knew they'd point the finger at me."

"So, Quinn questioned you, and you bought him off," I said.

"Yes. ... Yes, that's how it happened," Randy said.

"Where did the money come from for all this?" I said.

"My trust fund," Randy said.

"Not another word," Whittaker said.

"But you never killed him," I said.

"No, I swear to God," Randy said.

"Enough!" Whittaker shouted.

"O'Conner—did you pay him, too?" I said.

Randy looked to his father, then to me and ran out the door before anybody could stop him.

Merritt jumped up and gave chase. There was a long silence at the table.

Stewart looked to the stenographer. "Let the record show that Mr. Randall Rogers took flight in the middle of these proceedings," she said.

"Noticed that too, did you?" I said. "You got enough to go to the Grand Jury?"

"I do," Stewart said.

Merritt came back in to the room and took a seat. "Elevator door closed before I could get there." He was out of breath. "I phoned it in. He won't get far. They'll be waiting for him at his condo. Your place too, Rogers," he said.

The old man just sat there and never said a word. He bit his lip.

CHAPTER 57

We took Tiny's Maserati out to Cedar Junction, the three of us: Katharine Corbett up front with Tiny at the wheel and me in the back seat. It was time to let her son, Shawn, in on what was happening with his future. She was in another one of her tailored suits, and looked like she was on her way to her job at the bank—hard to believe that Shawn was her son. Genetics will always be a mystery to me.

"It's a miracle," Mrs. Corbett said.

"The truth has a way of coming out," I said.

"Yeah," Tiny said. "But in this case, Fenway here gave the truth a real hand up."

"I don't know how I'm ever going to thank you," she said, looking back at me. Her eyes were shiny.

I smiled and touched her shoulder. "Just did what I was paid to do. Thanks to Tiny, here." I said.

"Just so he stays out of trouble from here on in," Tiny added.

Katharine nodded quickly. "I hope to God he does," agreed Katharine.

"Might have been a real wake-up call for him," I offered. "Cedar Junction's no county lockup."

Suddenly Katharine blanched. "The knife fight—won't they hold him for the knife fight?"

I put my hand on her shoulder. "No charges filed; par for the course in there. Anyway, the guy's wounds were superficial."

She breathed a sigh of relief.

"He'll be looking for work," Tiny said. "I got a spot for him if there's nothing else lined up."

Katharine shot Tiny a look. "The idea is to keep him out of trouble, remember?"

Tiny laughed. "Nah, nothing like that, all on the up and up. There's this car dealer, he could work his way in as an apprentice mechanic."

"That's different," she said. She flashed Tiny a smile.

"How'd he react when you phoned him with the news?" I asked.

"I don't think it's sunk in yet," Katharine answered.

"Going to take a little time to get his feet on the ground," I said.

"An understatement," Tiny said.

"What will become of the Rogers boy?" Katharine asked.

"Still missing," Tiny said. "But he'll turn up soon enough. Not the kind of kid who'll stand up under questioning."

"He'll get a hell of a lot better representation than Shawn ever got," I said. "But he's going down."

Katharine just shook her head.

Shawn was still in chains, but we got to meet with him in the visitor's room rather than some windowless hole. There were vending machines, tables and views out to a broad field with a baseball diamond. A game was going on. The sun came streaming in through good-sized windows with no bars. Katharine gave him a hug and hung on for a very long time. No guard came forward to cut it off.

Tiny got Shawn a couple of candy bars and a Coke. We sat at a small round table while Shawn inhaled his treats and drained the last of his soda.

Tiny laughed. "You want some more?"

Shawn smiled and nodded eagerly. "Wouldn't believe what they feed us in here," he said.

"Got a pretty good idea," Tiny answered, then got up to make another trip to the vending machine.

"So, it's true?" Shawn said. "I'm really getting out of here?"

"It's true," Tiny told him.

"Caught a break," I said. "This new DA's willing to play ball. None of this mess happened on her watch."

"How long before I get sprung?" Shawn said.

"Two or three weeks," I said. "It takes a little time."

"I've got your old room all set for you, Shawn," Katharine said. "I didn't change a thing."

Shawn's eyes filled. He hugged her, doing the best he could with his shackles. Then he started to cry. "I've changed, Mom, honest I have. I'm off the dope," he said. "I swear."

"I've heard this all before, Shawn," Katharine said.

"But this time it's different," Shawn said.

"I hope so," she said. "I hope to God it is."

Tiny and I exchanged a look. Katharine was oblivious.

CHAPTER 58

Randy Rogers was missing for two full days before I got a courtesy call from Captain Merritt on my cell. A hiker had come across Randy on a nature trail at the Dover Country Club. The kid was on the ground, leaning against a tree. There was a half-empty vodka bottle beside him, and an empty bottle of Valium. The birds had wasted no time getting to him. His eyes had been pecked out, but his face was still recognizable. The raccoons had been working on his fingers. A couple of more days and the only way he could have been ID'd would have been by dental records.

There was bright yellow crime tape in a triangular pattern among the trees closing off the crime scene. Merritt saw me and waved me in. We watched as the lab boys did their thing.

"There's your perp," Merritt said.

"No sign of a struggle?" I asked.

Merritt shook his head. "No, the coroner will have the full

report by late tomorrow, but he's got all the signs of an overdose."

"Anybody see anything?"

"Yeah, caddy saw him walking out this way," Merritt said.

"Alone?"

"You got it," Merritt said. "You think O'Conner had anything to do with this?"

"Not his MO. Besides, nothing in it for him; the kid already spilled his guts."

"Yeah, there's that."

A lab man took pictures at all the usual angles, and then Randy was zipped into a body bag.

"Case closed," Merritt said.

"Looks that way," I said. "Think I'm going to nose around some, though."

"Be my guest. I'm out of here."

I headed for the clubhouse, and got the guided tour of the locker room from an older fellow with a fringe of snow-white hair and a well-trimmed mustache.

"Damn shame," he said.

Randy's locker was more like an oversized walk-in closet. A couple of techs were bagging articles of clothing and doing a general inventory—all very routine, no stone left unturned.

Tennis gear and a number of trophies hung on the wall. There were pictures of the kid everywhere poolside. Apparently he was the club's top swimmer and held the record in freestyle.

"Kid was an athlete," I said aloud.

"Tops," he replied.

"Never would have guessed it."

One of the techs opened up the built-in wooden cabinets, one at a time. The one on the end got my attention. I recognized the gleaming alligator bag instantly. There was a full complement of clubs all wrapped in tissue paper, and matching golf shoes still in the box.

"Okay if I have a look at these?" I asked the tech.

"You're with Merritt, right?"

"Right."

He handed me some surgical gloves. "Put these on."

I pulled every single club out, and gave each the once-over. They'd never been used. The shoes were in the same condition. The clubs weren't similar to those I'd seen on my visit to the Simpson house—they were identical. "Kid have another set of clubs anywhere?" I asked.

"Nope, not his game at all."

"That a fact. Damned expensive equipment for a guy who doesn't play."

"His father tried to get him into it, but nothing doing," the attendant said. "Father picked them up in Scotland."

"The kid never played in Scotland?"

"Never played anywhere. Hated the game. Hasn't been to Scotland since he was in grammar school."

"What about the old man?"

"Gets over there all the time—has what they call a golf villa, almost right on the fairway of St. Andrews."

"The old man. Not the kid," I said under my breath.

"Huh?"

"Like that man says: light dawns on Marblehead. Guess I'm

not such a hotshot detective after all."

"What?"

"Nothing. You've been very helpful." I put my hand on his shoulder. "Thanks for your time." I peeled off the rubber gloves and took my leave.

The attendant gave me a funny look.

CHAPTER 59

Merritt helped me on with the wire. I had to put it on over my Kevlar vest.

"You think Rogers will actually see you?" he said.

"Said he would."

"Doesn't make any sense, he's in the clear."

"Yeah, but I'm a loose end."

Merritt nodded. "And he doesn't like loose ends."

"Doesn't much like me, either."

"Yeah, there's that," Merritt said. "You get in any trouble, we'll be close by."

"Good to know."

A tech tested my wire. It worked perfectly. I was set to go.

Rogers answered the door himself. He looked me up and down, then stepped aside to let me in. He led me into the library, poured himself a scotch and took a seat in a leather wing chair. He held the drink in his left hand and pointed to a chair opposite him with his right. I continued to stand.

"This won't take long," I said.

"Damn right it won't," he said.

"You're done, Rogers. I know everything."

He got red in the face, but kept his cool and took a sip of his drink. "You're getting tiresome, Burke. Just what do you think you know?"

"It was you all along," I said. "You killed Simpson and paid a hit to cover it up."

"Ridiculous," Rogers said. "Randy admitted to paying off the policeman. Why would he do that if he hadn't killed the boy?"

"Because you told him he'd be the primary suspect. Not hard for the cops to find witnesses who saw them have words at the bar. Your son had no idea you were seeing him, too," I said.

Rogers shook his head. "You're a maniac, you know that? I met the boy once. Just once. Couldn't stand him."

"That why you took him to Scotland?"

There was a sheen on Rogers' forehead. His breath was ragged. He looked like he'd been gut-punched.

"He threatened to out you," I said.

His eyes went dull and he took a long pull on his scotch.

"He threatened to out you," I said again.

No response.

"Rogers?"

"You've got nothing, Burke."

"You think?"

"I know."

I made a face. "Aw, give it a rest, will you, Rogers? It'll be easy enough putting you in Scotland with Simpson. Somebody had to have seen you there together."

"And what does that prove?"

"Proves you knew him a hell of a lot better than you let on."

"So?"

"So right now, the case is closed. Maybe it gets opened again. Maybe people start asking you questions you don't want to answer. I figure it might be worth something to you to have me keep my mouth shut."

Rogers looked at me as if he were seeing me for the very first time.

"You want to blackmail me."

"That's one way of putting it."

"How much?"

"Not enough to put any real crimp in your style, but enough for me to not have to worry about anything. It can all go away."

"Interesting."

"Hell, *I'll* go away. Been missing those coconut palms."

"I had other plans for you, Burke, but we might be able to come to an accommodation."

"Thought we might. But you're going to have to come clean with me, all the way clean."

"The details are no concern of yours, as long as you get paid."

"Call it professional curiosity if you like. But we have no deal until I know those details. I've spent too much time on this one, putting the pieces together."

"Burke, you're a pain in my ass."

"My mission in life."

Rogers pursed his lips.

I glanced at my watch. "Haven't got all day."

Rogers settled back in his easy chair. "I gave him money."

"But he wanted more," I said.

Rogers stared off into nowhere. "It was an indiscretion. Never happened before," he said. "I'm not that way at all. I still don't know how it ever happened."

"You're human," I said.

Rogers nodded absently, his eyes lowered.

"He just might have gotten what he deserved," I said.

Rogers looked up. "He left me no choice," he said.

"So, you killed him."

Nothing from Rogers.

"Rogers."

"I suppose at this point it doesn't matter. You cross me, I can have you killed anytime I want."

"I'm not that easy to kill; might make more sense just to pay me off."

"Possibly."

"Either way, you still haven't answered my question."

Nothing.

"So?"

Yes, yes, I killed him. Are you happy now?"

"Ecstatic."

"You're a very irritating man. You know that, Burke?"

"Of course," I said.

"How much do you want?"

"I don't want your money, Rogers."

"But you—"

"I lied," I said.

Rogers' lips grew thin. "Back to Plan A, then," he said.

"Whatever you say, but I got a question for you. Randy was your only son. If it came right down to it, would you have let him take the fall for you?"

Rogers didn't respond at first, then his face contorted in a snarl. He exploded out of his chair, tossed his drink aside and reached inside his jacket. My shot caught him in the middle of the forehead just as he pulled his pistol. His head snapped back and he went down hard. The room reverberated with the single shot, then dead silence. I stood over the body.

"Man was a fool. I was supposed to do the job."

I turned slowly with my pistol raised. O'Conner stood in the doorway, using Rogers' Irish shillelagh for support. He had a thirty-eight on me.

"I knew you'd be here," I said.

"Could have shot you in the back," he said.

"You don't work for free," I said.

"Ah, boyo, there's the pity of it all. You just killed my meal ticket."

Our pistols were trained on one another. "Thought he'd have you right next to him."

"He wanted to talk to you first, told me to keep out of sight until he called me," O'Conner said. "Things didn't go the way he wanted, I was to blow you away. Had me by the door the whole time."

"Looks like he should have called you a little sooner," I said.

O'Conner smiled. "His call; stupid of me, I should have had him pay up front." He smiled at me.

I didn't return the smile.

"He hired you? Not the kid?"

"I never met the kid. My only contact was the old man."

"You'll have to answer for it."

O'Conner gave me a look. "I thought we had an understanding."

"When you escaped all bets were off."

"Things changed. You couldn't very well expect me to spend the rest of my life in a British prison, could you?"

"Not my problem," I said. "Besides, I couldn't let you off now if I wanted to. They'll be here any second. There's no way out for you."

Neither one of us spoke for a very long minute. Then he smiled. "You're wearing a wire, aren't you?"

I nodded.

"So I gave you what you wanted after all."

"The place is surrounded."

"I won't be taken alive," O'Conner said.

"Don't be a idiot," I said.

He smiled, feinted to his left but went to his right and fired. I made my move the same instant he did, turning my body at an angle to make a smaller target. I saw him wince. His bad leg slowed him just enough. His shot caught me high in the left arm. Mine caught him dead center in the middle of his throat. He grabbed for the wound. Blood gushed out and down his front. His mouth moved but no words came out. He looked me right in the eye and held my gaze. He fell first to his knees, then flat on his face. He twitched once, and then lay there very still.

I half-sat, half-fell into the leather wing chair Rogers had occupied just a few minutes before. Blood ran down my sleeve. It was just a nick but I felt a little faint.

The front door burst open and the room was filled with a dozen cops in body armor. Merritt brought up the rear.

CHAPTER 60

Megan and I planned a cruise up the coast of Maine, and I spent the morning getting things ship-shape on the *Whiffersnapper*. Afterward, I decided to treat us to a movie and a beer. I must have two hundred DVDs, from *Gone with the Wind*, to all the Marx Brothers, a dozen W.C. Fields and, believe it or not, *Who Killed Roger Rabbit*. I do love a good detective story. I tend to play some a hell of a lot more than I play others, though.

I laughed at myself as I selected an old friend and popped myself a beer. It was *Casablanca*. Megan would laugh at me too, but she wouldn't mind. Turns out, it's one of her favorites, too. I plugged it in when she got back from shopping. We were halfway through it when there was a commotion on deck and the dogs went nuts. I put it on pause. Tiny stuck his head through the hatch and came down the stairs with a six-pack of Heineken.

"Hear you guys are going on a boat ride," he said. "Thought

I'd come by and wish you '*bon voyage*.'" He handed me a beer and offered one to Megan.

She demurred. "I've been putting on a little weight," she said.

I wasn't worried about my weight.

"Glad you did," I said. I popped the can and clinked it to his.

"How long you going to be gone?" he asked.

"Hadn't really thought about it," I said. "Month, maybe two. Lots of islands off the coast of Maine."

Megan stood up. "You'll have to excuse me. I've got something I need to take care of—girl stuff."

"Want me to stop the action?" I said.

"No, don't bother," she said. "I'll be a while." She headed for our stateroom.

"What ya watching?" Tiny came around and looked at the screen for himself. Bogie was frozen in the middle of a conversation with Sidney Greenstreet. "Might have known." He polished off his beer, popped a new one and then sat next to me as I turned it back on.

"You're willing to sit through this?" I said.

He crinkled his brow. "Don't think I ever saw this part," he said.

"Seriously?" I said.

Tiny laughed and messed my hair. "Hey, I'm not as big a nut as you two are."

"That's a matter of opinion."

We sat through it all the way up to Ingrid Bergman's farewell scene with Bogie at the airport, and then I shut her down.

"Well, what did you think?" I asked.

Tiny shook his head. "Wouldn't sit through it a thousand times, but it was one hell of a flick."

"Grows on ya," I said.

"Bogie kinda reminds me of you."

"Take that as a compliment."

"'Cept you got the girl," Tiny said.

"Yep, I'm one up on him. Freed an innocent man to boot."

"Yeah, right," Tiny said, and then he gave me a look. "You haven't heard, have ya?"

"Heard what?" I said.

"Back in again," Tiny said.

I put down my beer and looked at him.

"He hasn't been out a week."

"Four days," Tiny said. "Picked up with more than an ounce of crack, got him for intent."

"Got to hand it to him, your kid brother didn't waste any time," I said.

"Can't choose your relatives," Tiny said. "With his record and that quantity, it's federal. You know their guidelines."

"He'll get a thousand years," I said.

"Something like that," Tiny said.

"Perfect," I said. "Just perfect."

Tiny threw back the rest of his beer and grabbed another, then slapped me on the back.

"Not like either one of us thought he'd become a Mormon. Don't think even his mom thought he would."

"Guess not."

"Anyway, you cracked the case. That's what I paid you for."

"Right, gives a fella a real sense of accomplishment," I said.

"Hey, I kept my promise to my dad and you did your job. At least the punk's going down for something he actually did. Besides, if it hadn't been for Shawn you never would have met Megan."

"Yep ... true enough. Ought to send him a thank-you note."

"Damn right," Tiny said.

We both looked up as Megan finally returned. She held up a small piece of white plastic. "It turned blue," she said, and gave me a huge smile.

She caught me completely off-guard. I put down my beer. "Blue?"

Tiny got up and whopped me on the back. "She's knocked up, you moron. Congratulations!"

I was speechless. Megan laughed.

"How'd that ever happen?" I finally managed.

"How do you think?" she asked.

"We'll have to get married," I announced.

"We're not in high school," Megan said. "We don't *have* to do anything."

"You don't want to get married?"

"Didn't say that, did I?" She smiled at me. "Girl's got to consider all her options, you know."

"Ah ... so that's how it is, huh?"

"You haven't even asked me yet."

I took another sip of my beer and settled back in my chair.

"So ... will ya?"

"Oh, Tiny," she said. "He's sweeping me off my feet."

"I wouldn't rush into anything if I were you," Tiny said. "He ain't much to look at."

"I'll really have to think this one over," Megan said. She took a seat on the couch.

I got up and went down on one knee, then two, and I took her hand and looked up at her.

"Megan, I'm down on both knees. I'll crawl on my belly if that's what it takes. You're my world. I need you in my life. I love you. Will you marry me?"

Her eyes filled, but she gave me one of her little trademark mischievous smiles.

"Well, that is an improvement. I'll give you that," she said.

"Listen you've got to look at the big picture. Don't set your sights too high. Remember, you're not getting any younger, and there's not that many men out there. You in, or what?"

She got up and gave me a little kiss on the forehead. "Well ... since you put it *that* way."

I made an aside to Tiny and mouthed: "Pushover."

"What's that?" Megan said.

"Nothing, dear, nothing at all. Tiny, you wanna be my best man?"

"Check my calendar."

"I'm going to make a sandwich. You two want anything?" Megan asked, heading for the galley.

"Ham and cheese would go good," Tiny said.

"You, darling?"

"Sure, I'll have one while you're in there. Oh, and Megan, take your shoes off will ya? Try to get into the spirit of the thing!"

"Don't make me reconsider, you!"

"Too late, I already booked the hall!"

EPILOGUE

Seven and one-half months later, in the waiting room of the North Shore Medical Center, Salem, Massachusetts, 11:13 a.m.

Tiny showed up four hours after I took her to the hospital and caught me in the waiting room.

"What are you doing here?" he said. "Thought you'd be in the delivery room with her."

"She had other plans," I said.

"Kicked you out?"

"Did me a favor. Thought I was having a rougher go of it than she was."

Tiny shook his head and took a seat next to me.

There were a half-dozen other guys hanging around, too. Tiny and I stood up as a young doctor entered the room.

"Mr. Ivanonavich?" he said.

"That's me," a guy on the other side of the room said, as he came over to the doc.

"Congratulations," the doc said.

We sat back down. "That guy just got here, for crying out loud," Tiny said.

"Tell me about it," I said. "Hope to God she's okay in there."

"They'd tell us if there was a problem—wouldn't they?"

"Got me—I sure as hell hope so!" I said.

We waited another two hours. Three more dads got the good word. I picked up my magazine for the two-thousandth time and put it right back down.

A little old doctor in a white coat came in. We hadn't seen him before. He had thinning white hair, and was a little stooped over. He looked to be in his early seventies at least.

"Mr. Burke?" he said.

I jumped to my feet, Tiny at my side, and rushed over.

"That's me," I said.

"Congratulations, Mr. Burke, you have a fine new baby girl."

He caught me off guard with that one. For some reason, Megan didn't want to know for sure in advance, but was convinced it would be a boy. That made two of us. I recovered and grabbed his hand with both of mine and shook it vigorously.

"Everybody all right?"

"Mother and daughter are doing just fine," the doc said.

"Took forever," I said.

"She was in labor for sixteen hours. We finally had to do a C-section." The doc smiled. "Don't worry, she told us she wanted to wear a bikini. The incision won't show."

I nodded. "When can I see her?"

"She's still sleeping. The delivery was a bit taxing on her, but you can see your daughter. That young lady's caused quite a stir with the nurses," the doc said.

"But there's nothing wrong, right?" I said.

"Far from it. They're starting a fan club; she's beautiful."

I broke into a laugh, slapped the doctor on the back and put on my very best Irish brogue. "And what would you be expecting?" I said.

"I'd be looking for a paternity test if I was you," the big man said, laughed and whopped me on the back so hard he almost knocked me off my feet.

"Yeah, yeah." I turned to the doc. "Surrounded by assassins," I said.

They were three deep by the door when we got there—not just nurses, but new mothers as well, with their own newborns in their arms and craning their necks to get a look at *my* new arrival, all "oohs" and "ahhs."

The doc spoke up. "Clear the way, the father's here."

Megan was still under, oblivious. The nurse handed me my new baby girl. She was an absolute mirror image of Megan. It was uncanny. She had Megan's thick dark brown hair and plenty of it. Someone had gathered it up and put a big pink bow on her. Megan's eyes, Megan's olive skin, even her smile, though the doc said it had to be just gas. There was none of the Burke side at all. She was all Griffin.

She grabbed my thumb and held on tight. I was instantly in love. "Jesus," I said.

A new mother by the door looked up. "*You're* the father?" she said.

"That's the rumor, yeah," I said.

"Kid's a clone," Tiny said. "What? You phone this one in or something?"

The new mother blushed and gave me a huge smile, then touched my arm. "Well, congratulations," she said, as she rocked her own child in her arms. "With the exception my own little boy here, she's the most beautiful baby in the world."

"Thanks," I said. "Thanks so much, but she's her mother's little girl. Looks like I've been cut out of the loop."

"You can say that again," Tiny said.

"Right," I said. "All Megan and none of me."

"Kid caught a real break there," Tiny said.

"Hard to argue with that one," I said.

"But you was looking for a boy, weren't cha?"

I rocked her gently in my arms and planted a kiss on her fore head, my eyes filling.

"She'll do just fine," I said. "Just fine."

CPSIA information can be obtained at www.ICGtesting.com
Printed in the USA
LVOW101319091112

306643LV00001B/1/P